When James stopped believing

When James stopped believing

A story of love, lies and honesty

By Matthew King

ISBN (paperback) 9781838317508

ISBN (ebook) 9781838317515

For Peter – who introduced me to the journey.

CHAPTER 1

The sermon had gone well. Earnest faces looked engaged and many members of the congregation smiled at the lighter moments of James' talk. He had brought verses from the Old Testament book of Isaiah to life for a 21st century congregation – "I was found by those who did not seek me, I revealed myself to those who did not ask for me." Words written nearly three thousand years ago yet James had skilfully related them to the modern world. Putting modesty aside, he might even have described it as one of his best sermons. It was deeply ironic therefore that this was the moment when James knew he had to stop being a church minister. As he made his way down the stone steps from the pulpit, he could not shake off the overwhelming feeling that all of this – church, the Bible, faith - was simply a work of human wishful thinking. Thirty years old, in full time ministry

1

since leaving college, the Reverend James Chambers reached the bottom of the familiar descent and admitted to himself, "My faith has gone."

After the service many of the congregation stayed for refreshments and several chatted to James, commenting on the sermon or mentioning problems they had. However James was barely listening as the consequences of his revelation began to sink in. If this sudden absence of belief persisted and if he wanted to remain honest with himself (and he had always been honest with himself), he would have to give up the enjoyable and satisfying life he had carved out and find a "proper" job. He had no idea what else he could possibly do.

James had wanted to become a church minister since the age of 15. Church had always been a part of his family's routine and James had friends there, so he continued going without protest at an age when other teenagers might have opted out, either through reasoned argument or, more likely, by turning Sunday morning into a battleground for parents who were eventually relieved to attend without the sulky presence. His older brother Peter had taken this option. He had made Sunday morning such an unpleasant time for his parents that eventually they relented and attended with just James in tow. Like many parents they accepted that their children were simply different. Whilst Peter was ambitious, worldly and interested in money-making from an early age, James was more of a dreamer. They also looked different. Peter was stocky and good-looking in spite of his fairly rugged appearance, whereas James had a wiry frame and more delicate features. As he continued to listen distractedly to his parishioners, James had a rare moment of wishing he were more like his brother. In a situation like this, Peter would be decisive; agonising was not in his nature. In fact he would probably have found a way of making money from the dilemma and left the church without a second thought. However, James was not like his brother. At the age of 30, after eight years in full-time ministry, James would have to work out his own way of dealing with this totally unexpected crisis of faith.

CHAPTER 2

The interview with Bishop John went surprisingly well. James hadn't been looking forward to it but felt he owed John an explanation, rather than just sending a letter of resignation through the post. He had predicted some of John's responses – "we all have doubts at times", "this may just be a phase you need to work through", "how is your own devotional time?" However, James was convinced this was not a passing phase. He even tried to lighten the mood by talking about a "reverse Road to Damascus experience" but maybe, on reflection, that was ill judged. They agreed James would continue in post for six months and that he would not tell anyone yet about his decision. He would use guest preachers as often as he could and focus more on listening than providing answers when people came to him with big questions. This was the area James was most concerned about. It was easier to play a role in public than in private, and he was known as a minister who was approachable and even relished debate.

When he arrived home from seeing Bishop John, James noticed his garden looked particularly neat and that Stan was on his doorstep.

"Time for a cup of tea, vicar?" Stan asked.

"Of course, Stan. I see you've been busy. Great job as usual. The least I can do is give you a cup of tea."

"Just glad I can do something to help a young man doing such important work. Nothing more important than telling people about God, is there?"

Stan was a man of means, in his fifties, with no need to work again. He dropped by once a week to look after James' garden, and tended to stay long enough to catch the young vicar for a chat. Stan was single and probably lonely, and James usually enjoyed his conversations with him. This particular afternoon, though, was not the most convenient for James as he was after a bit of time to reflect on his conversation with the Bishop.

"Been out with your vicar friends?" Stan asked as they sat at the kitchen table, tea and biscuits to hand.

"No, I've been to see the Bishop."

"Oh yes, one of those performance appraisals, I'll bet. We used to have them in my company. Made no difference at all, of course, people just made up stuff so they could get their next pay rise. I always knew who was working hard and who wasn't, but we had to go through all that nonsense. Would have been better without it, of course, just let people concentrate on the work."

"Well, we try to be honest, the Bishop and I," James said.

"Suppose it's a bit different in the church. How do you know if someone's doing a good job? It's not as simple as bums on seats, is it? Do you think the Bishop sends someone to listen to your sermons?"

"I don't think so, Stan. I think he relies on me telling him like it is. If I have any issues, I will be open with him."

"That's good. Do you have any issues at the moment?"

"I've always admired your directness, Stan," James said with a smile, "but I'm sure you'll understand there could be questions of pastoral confidentiality here."

"You mean I need to mind my own business. Must be lonely as a vicar, though, what with no wife to talk things through with. I know Saint Paul wasn't a big fan of wives, but maybe he'd met some tricky women."

"One Corinthians seven 'Now to the unmarried and the widows I say: It is good for them to stay unmarried, as I do'," James quoted the Bible from memory. "I read that as Paul saying that a wife could have got in the way of his work, that he may not have been a good husband because of what he was doing. I'm not sure it applies to all men everywhere."

"Good to hear you're keeping your options open."

This was a favourite topic for Stan, who had never been married himself. James wasn't sure whether Stan was genuinely concerned to see him settle down with a wife, or whether he wanted a discussion on meeting women generally, in the hope that he might still find a partner. Either way it was not an area James wished to debate in any detail with Stan.

"So, what else are you up to today, Stan?"

"Well, I'm popping into town in a bit. They're looking for volunteers at a new charity shop. I've got a bit of time on my hands, so I'd thought I'd go and talk to them."

Stan had actually been at a bit of a loss since he sold his business. After the initial euphoria of seeing a very healthy bank balance, he struggled to know what to do with his time that gave him challenge and interest. He had explored the charity option before but, having run his own company for years, he did not always cope with being told what to do. After Stan had tried to interfere once too often, the manager had suggested he might use his expertise elsewhere.

"You know they're likely to boss you around a bit," James said, hoping to prepare the way.

"I know what you're saying. That's why I like doing your garden. I just get on with it and you seem grateful."

After Stan had gone, James remembered he had some work to do for his next church event. Earlier in the year, in response to requests from the congregation, he had agreed to set up an evening called "How reliable is the Bible?" At the time it had seemed a good idea. It was now the last thing he wanted. Maybe he should rename it "How reliable is your vicar?"

CHAPTER 3

As he carried out his research on how the Bible was put together, James' mind turned again to the situation he found himself in. He thought about what had brought him to faith in the first place. One of the fascinating things about church for James as a teenager was the chance to hear adults talk about themselves and their experiences in a way he had not encountered elsewhere. This often related to how God had been at work in their lives or even how God had spoken to them. One of the older members of the congregation described how God had led him out of a life of crime as a young man (James felt his time in prison might have been a factor too), but also how God had helped him to let go of the anger he felt at his friend who had run off with all the stolen money and had never been seen again. It was a fascinating insight into the life of someone James only knew as the old man at the back with a scruffy beard and faded tattoos.

Sermons could be interesting too. Every week a group of about 100 people would listen as a few lines from a two-thousand-year-old book were examined and somehow related to life today. James had come across this in school assemblies in a very basic way – the Deputy Head would take an incident from Christ's life and explain (in a rambling way that always lasted exactly six minutes) that Jesus was really talking about how young people should sit quietly and behave on the school bus. This had become a standing joke at school, among staff and pupils, but the sermons at church were more robust. They felt as though they had thought and scholarship behind them – this was serious and important. The ideas mattered and James related to many of them.

School had also played a part in his decision to become a church minister. It was not something James would tell everyone at the time but his favourite lesson at school had been RE. He was fascinated by what people believed and by what they would do as a result of these beliefs – sometimes they would devote their lives to telling others and sometimes they would accept, even welcome, death rather than give up their beliefs. This was also the only lesson where there was genuine debate. The teacher was surprisingly relaxed in her approach and the most extreme views could be debated. He particularly enjoyed a debate on the criminally insane; the school was near a high security prison where the inmates were locked up for life because they had done horrendous things and could never be trusted in society. The class was questioning why these people should be looked after for years at great cost, and several pupils felt it would be better to kill them. It was such a waste of money and manpower to keep such evil people alive. James felt this was wrong but struggled to develop his arguments beyond "but we are human" or "this is not what a civilised society should do." He thought he might trump those in favour of death for the inmates by asking them directly, "Would you be happy to kill them and live with that for the rest of your life?" They all said yes without hesitation.

So being a vicar would allow him to explore issues and beliefs on a daily basis – and he would get paid for it. This was another factor in his decision – vicars got a regular income. It wasn't a great income but it seemed to be enough and often it came with a very nice house. James' father worked in sales and was clearly not satisfied with his job. Sometimes he would bring home a good salary and the family might enjoy an expensive holiday. But his father did not believe in what he was doing. The machines he was selling were not the best, but he had to pretend they were, and he was given ridiculously high sales targets. If he managed to meet them, he was congratulated and then given even higher ones. It made for a stressful life with many hours on the road and regular periods of unemployment. All in all, being a vicar seemed a far better choice.

So if he was now to give up being a vicar, what else would he do? He remembered completing an online test at school which indicated he should consider a career in social work or librarianship. He had then had an interview with an adviser and had mentioned the possibility of going into the church but her response had been rather discouraging.

"No one has ever said that to me before."

"Right." James was quite taken aback. "But people do become vicars."

"Yes, of course. But, well, why do you want to do that?"

"I think it would be interesting..."

James' answer tailed off and he realised he had some way to go before convincing anyone of his calling. He left the interview quite angry – it was as if the adviser was questioning the value of the work that vicars do, that helping people think through exactly what they believe and where they stand on issues was somehow less important than putting books back on the shelves in a library.

In the end James studied English at university. He wrote his dissertation on the metaphysical poets and enjoyed immensely the ideas and the way they were presented. However, Samuel Johnson's criticism that the poetry was intellectually but not emotionally stimulating did give him pause for thought. He had to admit he was more at home with ideas than feelings – in fact this notion went around in his head for weeks (which rather proved the point). He decided to broach it with one of the other students on the course. Melissa was also studying the metaphysical poets.

"Mel, do you think this poetry appeals to people who are academically good but emotionally a bit under-developed?"

Mel looked rather taken aback, and James realised it may not have been the best way to start the conversation.

"What are you trying to say, James?" Mel asked and the way she said his name suggested he was on dangerous ground.

"I mean, well, Johnson said something about them 'not being successful in representing or moving the affections' and I'm thinking about myself – whether I perhaps spend too much time in the world of ideas."

"You feel strongly about some things, though, don't you?"

"I feel strongly about ideas and the freedom to debate them."

"Hmm. Maybe Samuel Johnson had a point. Have you ever been in love?"

"Not sure."

James had never been in love. He'd read about the feeling of panic and excitement when someone entered the room, of rehearsing various things to say and never being satisfied with any of them, of deciding in the end to say something really simple and sounding a bit stupid, of trying not to stare but ending up not being able to look anywhere else. He was fascinated by this aspect of human experience but it was, for James at this stage in his life, just another interesting concept.

Maybe Mel had a point and it was coming back to haunt him all these years later. Had he based his life choices on mere ideas rather than a passion or a calling, and were his choices therefore bound eventually to unravel? And yet he would surely never have got this far if he hadn't had some sort of depth of conviction.

Training for the ministry had been a bit like university, but with regular services and prayers. James believed in the basics of the Christian faith and enjoyed the debate around what his lecturers called secondary issues. There were many strongly held views on everything, from how services should be run to the role women should play in them, and James found himself relishing the regular discussions; it didn't bother him that he was not as passionate as some of his fellow ordinands on these matters. He could live with the ambivalence and this could be one of the reasons he got his first curacy. The church leaders appointing him had quoted from his Bible college reference – "James' ability to balance opposing views is impressive for one so young."

James knew that people sometimes talked about 'head knowledge' and 'heart knowledge' in Christian circles. Perhaps he'd gone a bit too far with the head knowledge and needed the passion that some Christians showed when talking about God. James frequently used set prayers in his personal devotional time. He loved the way the words often expressed what he was feeling with a succinct beauty. However, maybe it was time to open up a bit more and just pray exactly what was on his mind. So, before getting back to his planning for the church event, James got down on his knees and simply told God he didn't know if He was there – and he didn't know what to do. It all felt rather pointless but it couldn't hurt, he reasoned.

CHAPTER 4

One of the unusual things about being a vicar was having a day off in the week. James' free day was Thursday. This was fantastic in the summer as it was often the first day of a Test match and James got inordinately excited about seeing that first delivery bowled on a morning full of hope and excitement for cricket fans (particularly as most of the country was hard at work). At other times of the year, he enjoyed pottering around the local village on his day off. The charity shops were surprisingly well stocked – in fact they had got consistently better and busier over the years and the unwelcoming musty smell that used to mark them out from other shops had largely disappeared. Reading the paper sitting by the village pond or in one of the warm and busy coffee shops was a pleasure that he looked forward to.

"Yo, Vic!"

James turned to see the fifteen-year-old Jack, greeting him in his surprisingly upbeat manner.

"Morning, Jack."

"Is there porn in hell? I reckon there is as it's obviously not what God wants. Won't heaven be a bit boring? I'm just weighing up my options."

Jack was sharp, quick-witted and liked to get straight to the point. He was also a persistent truant, hence his presence in the village on a Thursday morning.

"We don't know exactly what hell will be like – but it's clear it will be bad," James explained.

"Best not to take the risk then?"

"Exactly."

"Still, I suppose you would say that, wouldn't you? It's like asking a BMW salesman about buying a Porsche. Do you think porn's bad?"

"Yes...."

"Why? The female body's a beautiful thing and God made it. You do think the female body is beautiful, don't you?"

"Yes, and as you say, God created it. But porn gets us to see people as objects rather than people so it's not right."

James had spent time with Jack on many occasions, trying to convince him that education was the way ahead – yes, there were boring lessons and some of the teachers were annoying, but skiving off school would limit future opportunities. Jack knew it all – he also knew his parents had no control over him and that doing as you were told was "not something he was into".

"Have you slept with a woman?" Jack asked, direct as ever.

"Now remember Jack – we've been over this before – I'm happy to talk about anything with you, but you have to respect that some questions are too personal."

The fact was James felt uncomfortable talking about this area of human experience. He remembered his university conversation about being "emotionally under-developed" and wondered whether this still applied to him. He had had sex at university but he thought of it as a fleeting pleasure rather than magical (fortunately he did not make this observation at the time). He certainly hadn't been in love; in fact he had never had a relationship that looked likely to turn serious.

19

"Anyway," he stood and turned to Jack, "get back off to school now or I'm telling your parents you were skiving again."

Jack rolled his eyes. They both knew this would make no difference.

"Yeah, sure!" Jack said, getting up and sauntering off in the right direction at least.

James felt a little down on himself as he went into his favourite coffee shop and ordered a cappuccino and a Danish pastry.

"Okay if I join you?"

James' mood lifted as he looked up to see Alice with her latte.

"Of course. How are you, Alice?"

"I'm fine. Got an hour before an interview so I thought I'd potter around town."

"I like a nice potter."

Alice was a freelance journalist. James was always interested in her work because she wrote the sort of articles that he liked to read.

"Who are you interviewing?" he asked her.

"A retired footballer – but not a top level one. I thought it would be interesting to see what a lower league player did after his sporting career was over. He wouldn't have made enough money to set himself up for life so he's going to have to work, but you'd think that anything would be a bit of a come down after following your passion for ten years."

"So what's he going to do?"

"I don't know," said Alice. "I'll ask him." And then she added with a smile, "Maybe he'll become a vicar."

"Really?"

"Would you recommend it?"

Perhaps it was the journalist in her but Alice often seemed to come out with questions that got to the heart of the matter. James was a little taken aback by having to answer such a direct challenge but hoped he didn't show it.

"You've got to want to do it," James managed to say.

"Obviously."

"It has variety and it gets to the very nub of human existence."

"Now there's a word you don't hear very often – nub," Alice was smiling again. "And I believe it also has a new meaning – someone who's not very good at video games. I heard it recently – my nephew called his brother a nub."

"Are you sure it was nub?"

"Cheeky vicar," Alice said in mock admonishment.

James really enjoyed Alice's company. She was intelligent, interesting, funny, and, yes, good looking, particularly when she wore her jet black hair in a ponytail.

"What do you think you would have done if you hadn't become a vicar?" Alice asked casually.

James was beginning to get nervous. Was she that good a journalist she could sniff out a story just by looking at someone? Was she in with the Bishop? James decided to fight back with a question.

"Are you preparing an article on vicars now?"

"No," Alice smiled, "I was just wondering."

"That's what all journalists say. Anyway, probably not a footballer. I think I could rule out everything in the sporty and mathematical line; maybe a teacher, though the way the government insists on seeing education as something you can measure and put in league tables would depress me. I'm not sure...."

"But you've always wanted to work in the church...."

James smiled. "You are thinking of an article, aren't you?"

Alice held her hands up in mock defence. "No. Honestly! I'll move on. So, what else are you up to today?"

The exchange had been friendly and full of smiles and they continued chatting happily, but James wondered whether Alice had sensed something. He had promised Bishop John his decision would remain a secret. On the other hand the thought of talking it through with someone as sensitive, intelligent and considerate as Alice was suddenly very appealing. And, as far as he knew, Alice had a secure faith.

When James left the coffee shop, he noticed Jack sitting on the bench opposite.

"Hey, Vic, who's your fit friend?"

James ignored him.

CHAPTER 5

So, how reliable is the Bible? James could put it off no longer, he had to get down to some serious preparation work for the forthcoming church event which he now regretted agreeing to. He knew the evening could be hijacked by members of the congregation who had strong views, though not necessarily the same strong views. There were those who thought it important to take the Word of God seriously and literally (and they tended to condemn anyone who didn't). This group felt that if only we studied the Bible enough, we would have all the truth. On the other hand James was aware of those who felt that the Bible was there to be interpreted and that currently we only "see through a glass, darkly" (he thought that was from Paul's letter to the Corinthians, but he needed to check). There was the potential for tension between the two camps; the first group thought of the second group as wishy-washy liberals, whereas the second group regarded the first as unthinking literalists. This could be a tricky evening.

James was not too disappointed when his preparations were interrupted by the doorbell.

"Good morning, Reverend Chambers, I hope I am not disturbing you," said the serious young man on the doorstep. James did not recognise him.

"No, not at all, that's fine."

"My name is Simon and I am hoping to have a talk with you. There's a decision I'm wrestling … yes, wrestling with. It would be very helpful to talk to someone who is a good listener."

"Of course. Do come in."

James led Simon through to the kitchen where he offered him a drink. Simon politely refused. He was only here to talk. Having experienced some quirky individuals in churches he had attended, James was ready for just about anything. Simon was more earnest than nervous as he talked about what was on his mind.

"Do you know how many times the word "guide" is mentioned in the Psalms?" Simon asked.

"No, I don't know that."

"It is mentioned nine times. That's in the King James version of the Bible. And in the New International Version the figure is eleven."

"Are you looking for guidance at the moment?" James asked.

"Yes, indeed," Simon replied. "I am looking for guidance. Can you tell me how you think God guides us?"

Suddenly the preparation work for the church discussion on the reliability of the Bible was looking a more attractive option.

"I think God provides some overriding principles – through the Bible and through the way Jesus lived – and that we need to make decisions with these principles in mind. I think it's rare for God to guide very specifically; I think it is about living with reference to Him, in relationship with Him, if you like, rather than thinking of guidance as people being automatons who are controlled by God."

In the circumstances, James was quite pleased with this summary.

"So you do not believe in the Sovereignty of God?" Simon responded with a frown.

"I do," James responded. "God is all-knowing and all-powerful. However, he also gave us the ability to choose. We read in the Bible of God being unhappy with choices people make and holding them responsible for things they've done wrong. This doesn't mean he is not sovereign – I suppose it is a question of to what extent God applies His sovereignty. I think the bottom line is He wants a relationship with us, not to be a puppet-master."

"Hmm, that is interesting," said Simon and he sounded genuine. "So, do you think I should apply for the job at Ikea?"

"That's a bit of a jump, isn't it?"

"That is where I'm looking for guidance," Simon explained.

"Is there any reason why you shouldn't apply for the job at Ikea?" asked James.

"No. I cannot think of any reason."

"Then I would apply and see what happens. Sometimes it's a matter of testing things out and keeping that openness to God. Hopefully it will become clear whether it is the right decision."

"How will it become clear?"

James wondered about this young man in front of him for a moment. Simon was obviously familiar with church language. Perhaps he had already asked all these questions in his own church and for some reason was not happy with the answers.

"There are all sorts of ways it could become clear. You go for an interview and something puts you off; maybe you sense that their values don't fit with your own. On the other hand you may really like the manager and that could be a positive sign. I would just take it one step at a time and see what happens."

"A bit like Ecclesiastes."

"Ecclesiastes?" James asked – he hadn't read that particular book of the Bible in a while.

"Focus on what you are doing today – the future is the future," Simon explained.

"I would have to read Ecclesiastes again. It's been a long time....."

Simon abruptly got up to go.

"Thank you. This is very helpful," he said.

James was pleased this conversation had come to a positive end and he wondered again about what brought Simon here.

"Are you a member of a church at the moment?" he asked.

"Yes, I go to St Paul's."

James knew it well; it was the big Anglican church in the next town.

"And have you talked to them about this decision you have to make?"

"Yes, I have discussed this and other decisions with the vicar there. But he is away on a mini break at the moment."

James wondered whether the two things were connected and then admonished himself for being so uncharitable. Simon was a serious young man who needed support and encouragement.

"Well, it's been good to talk to you, Simon. I wish you luck with your job application."

"Oh," said Simon, looking shocked, "you believe in luck?"

"No, of course not, not at all. It's just an expression. I mean, I wish you all the best with your application."

"Thank you. Goodbye."

James watched as Simon left, walking down the drive with the well-kept flower beds on either side. He had a strange feeling that this would not be the last time he would see Simon.

As he tried to settle back down to his preparation for the forthcoming Bible evening, James could not shake off the feeling that he was living as a fraud. He thought back over what he had said to Simon. How much of it did he actually believe? Could he carry on like this for another six months? On the other hand Bishop John was right. James was not the first church minister to suffer a crisis of faith. Maybe in the next few weeks he would step down from the pulpit after a sermon and suddenly be struck by the truth of it all. A knee jerk reaction now could lead to much regret in the future. James had always been quite independent but he was suddenly feeling in desperate need of a friend, someone he could open up to. However, confiding in anyone would be very dangerous and go against what he had agreed with the Bishop. Perhaps he could talk to someone about his situation as if talking about someone else - "I have a friend who is a vicar but he has recently lost his faith." That sounded so obvious. No, he needed to be a bit more creative.

CHAPTER 6

"So, you think I would make a good vicar?!" Alice stared at James incredulously.

"Yes, I think you would. I'm not saying you should, I just wonder whether it is something you have considered."

"Never."

James' plan was not going well. As they had discussed careers last time they met, he thought it would be logical to ask Alice about whether she could imagine being a church minister - just casually, in passing - and the following discussion might then allow him to talk about some of the issues he was facing. And this might help him in his current predicament. Instead he was faced with a starey, stunned woman. Interestingly even the starey, stunned look did not make her any less attractive. James moved on quickly from this thought and tried to rescue the situation.

"I mean, it was just off the top of my head. You have a faith, you are good with people, you are intelligent…"

"Yes, but to be a vicar is a calling. You have to have a conviction it's the right thing to do – something to carry you through the tough times."

This sounded a bit more promising to James. Could she perhaps develop this idea, throw in a few tips as to how to handle a situation like this?

"And I have not had the slightest inkling of a conviction like that."

This was less promising.

"Okay, well, forget I mentioned it. It was a bit random, I admit."

"Random and bizarre," Alice concluded.

James sensed Alice's journalistic mind working. Had she rumbled him? He knew Alice would not simply accept this episode on face value. He knew her work, had discussed many of her articles with her and knew that she was tenacious and forensic when it came to getting at the truth. He felt this Saturday morning coffee (again "casually" suggested by him), could turn out to be a big mistake.

"Actually, I have been thinking about your job," Alice announced, apparently moving on.

"Really?"

"Yes, after our last coffee where you were worried I was interviewing you. Well, it got me thinking. Maybe an article about what a vicar actually does would be quite interesting. Everyone knows what he gets up to on Sunday, but what about the rest of the week? Does he meditate, does he play golf, does he share a sauna with unbelievers?"

James' heart sank. His plan to find support in his hour of need was quickly turning into Alice's plan to get to the truth of what was going on. Alice continued with her thoughts on the article and James wondered how he could stop her.

"I could perhaps sit in on one of your chats with someone from the congregation. I hear you are very good in that situation. We could talk about the challenge of getting going every morning when you haven't got an office to go to. And then keeping a church together where people have opposing views on things like same-sex marriage. What do you think?"

"Another latte?"

James joined the thankfully long queue at the counter to wait for more coffee and to consider his response. Much as he wanted to, he could not talk openly with Alice. That would be wrong. If she did write an article about him, it could end up being about a vicar losing his faith. That would be even more wrong. He had promised Bishop John he would tell no one ("sorry, Bishop, I may just have mentioned it to a journalist who has written it up as a fascinating article for a popular magazine and website. Don't know what came over me.") He would have to say no. As he reached this conclusion, he realised he was disappointed. And he was disappointed because he would be turning down the opportunity to spend a lot more time with Alice. Eventually he heard her voice.

"They're asking you what you want."

It seems the barista had asked him three times for his order and James had not responded. Alice had eventually come over to help out.

"Are you okay?" she asked, as they sipped their second coffees.

"Yes, I was just deep in thought about your idea."

"I think people would be interested. Are you worried about confidentiality? I could change names and obviously ask permission if I am writing about sensitive issues." Alice seemed enthusiastic.

"It's, um… well…," James was struggling. He could usually think on his feet but the only honest thing he could do would be to stand up and announce to the whole coffee shop, "This marvellous, clever, determined and perceptive woman is going to see through me. It's just a question of time."

James' thoughts were interrupted by a hearty greeting from Bernard, and for once James was pleased to see him.

"Morning, James! How are you?" (It was a rhetorical question, as always with Bernard.) "Looking forward to your evening on the Bible. It's very important to get that right, otherwise what is our faith based on?"

"Morning, Bernard. Ah, yes, I'm hoping it will be an encouraging discussion."

"Yes," agreed Bernard. "Although I'm not sure there's much to discuss, the Bible is the word of God. Full stop."

James took his cue from "full stop" to change the subject.

"Are you off to the rugby this afternoon?" he asked.

"Yes, though woe betide them if they haven't sorted their lineout. Last week was a disgrace – you'd think they don't practise! How difficult is it to throw a ball in a straight line to a man who jumps and catches it?" (Another rhetorical question – and, in any case, not one that James felt qualified to answer). "Enjoy your coffee."

Bernard moved on. If James had not been a vicar, it would have been a perfect moment to share a smile with Alice. However, James knew he was never fully off duty, so he retained his poker face.

"Do you think he says other punctuation types when he wants to make a different sort of statement?" Alice wondered, also with a straight face. She understood the rules of coffee with the local vicar.

"Sorry?"

"Well, 'full stop' clearly means 'there is no chance that what I have just said is wrong'. Do you think he uses 'semi-colon' when he is less sure?" Alice explained.

"I don't think he's ever less sure. Bernard tends to be right. Full stop."

Enough time had now passed to allow them to smile.

CHAPTER 7

James was usually keen to see plenty of people at church events. It was not a particularly reliable indicator of how effective he was in his role, but it was only human to be encouraged by a good crowd. However, the church evening on "How reliable is the Bible?" was an exception. James was not looking forward to it, and if he had waited alone in an empty church hall before concluding that no one was interested, he would have returned home a relieved man. However, the attendance was remarkably good. Did members of the congregation want to learn about how to approach the Bible – or had they already made up their mind and were now just looking for a good argument?

If he had a list of people he would most like to see coming through the door, Alice would be at the top. And Bernard would be at the bottom. So, things were not going well.

Bernard had arrived early, keen to get a good seat, and Alice had not appeared at all, even though the advertised starting time had now passed. This was very unusual for Alice. One of the many things James liked about her was her reliability – she always did what she said she was going to do. James felt even more uneasy about the evening.

Though this made it obvious he was expecting a tense evening, James started with some verses from the first letter to John from the New Testament about love, focussing in particular on chapter four verse eight, "Whoever does not love does not know God, because God is love." He said that love was more important than argument and clever words. He mentioned that the word "love" was used forty-three times in this particular book of the Bible. The visit from Simon had clearly had an effect and as he looked up, James noticed Simon sitting at the back. He had been right about seeing him again. Having effectively warned everyone to be nice to each other, James then gave some background on the Bible. He explained that it was made up of sixty-six books and outlined the variety of types of writing contained within the books. To illustrate his point he quoted a few lines from the Song of Songs, which could be seen as a love poem and made some quite overt references to the beauty of the human body. His mind inevitably turned to Alice. Where was she? He explained that there were arguments over other books, the Apocrypha, which some Christian denominations include in the Bible and others merely see as useful, but not Holy Scripture.

The evening moved on to discussing questions in small groups. James joined different groups, saying as little as he could get away with. Bernard inevitably dominated his group but Stan was also there and he was not one to sit back quietly. Both agreed that everyone interprets the Bible to some extent, not taking every word literally, with Stan quoting Jesus' words, "And if your eye causes you to sin, tear it out."

"Would anyone do that?" Stan asked.

Simon was in a different group and concentrating intently. James did not hear him contribute but could almost sense that he was storing up a list of questions that would come out in future. Still, this was the point of the evening – an opportunity to reflect on the potentially difficult issue of how people see the Bible. In previous centuries people had been put to death for their views on the Bible, so it was, on reflection, quite brave to hold an event like this, James told himself.

"What about this verse? 'Women should remain silent in the churches. They are not allowed to speak, but must be in submission, as the law says. [35] If they want to inquire about something, they should ask their own husbands at home; for it is disgraceful for a woman to speak in the church'."

Bernard posed the question during the q and a session at the end. James knew this would potentially be the most difficult part of the evening and had even wondered about just sticking to discussion groups, but he knew he would never get away with that.

"Oh, come on, Bernie ..." This was Barbara, one of the women who knew Bernard well – well enough to know that he hated being called Bernie.

"At least use my proper name if you want to address me," Bernard interrupted. "Maybe this is why Paul had to write to the church in Corinth, because there were women who liked to stir things up..."

James knew he had to step in.

"Wait a moment. Let's have a think about this. We're into a whole new issue here. You raise a very important question, Bernard – are there parts of the Bible which relate more to the time when they were written than they do to us today? To be frank, that is a whole new discussion that we could devote another evening to." (Maybe next year when there was a new vicar).

"Yes, but what do you think, James?" Bernard's directness always won out over any awareness of another person's discomfort.

"I think there are verses in the Bible which refer to issues of the time. In Ephesians we read the advice to slaves, 'Slaves, obey your earthly masters with respect and fear'. I don't think the Bible condones slavery but these words appear to address believers in a society where it was the norm. So you could argue that this verse requires some interpretation. And the words you quote, Bernard, may have been addressed to a church where there was a specific problem. When discussing these verses, to balance them out if you like, some would also refer to Deborah, who led the Israelites in the Old Testament, as an example of a woman taking a traditionally male role with God's blessing."

James was speaking quickly now to try to avoid any further interruptions.

"Interestingly this passage comes straight after the chapter which is all about love being far more important than anything else – 'if I can fathom all mysteries and all knowledge, ... but do not have love, I am nothing'. Anyway, time is getting on. Thank you all for coming; it has been good to think about these issues but we really ought to close now."

And James launched into a closing prayer before anyone else could interrupt.

As people shuffled out, conversing quietly (possibly about the Bible, but more likely about Bernard), James felt relief that the evening was over but also a renewed concern that he had not heard from Alice. Inevitably, Bernard stopped for a word before leaving.

"I noticed you ducked that question about women at the end," he said to James.

James tried to maintain a patient and calm tone in his answer.

"It's such a big issue, Bernard, we really couldn't have done it justice right at the end of a long evening of debate."

"That's as maybe, but I look forward to an evening where we can talk about it properly. There's no harm in a spot of proper debate. I think some people don't like to hear opposing views. It's not very fashionable to disagree but I think it's healthy."

"Yes, I agree, but I think on certain issues there will be always be a range of views."

"There may be a range of views but some of them will be wrong. And by debating them we can get at the truth," Bernard countered. "I tell you who likes to get at the truth, it's that friend of yours, Alice. I've read some of her articles – she doesn't mess about."

CHAPTER 8

James hadn't slept well. There was the worry about Alice not turning up to the meeting, without an explanation. And then there were Bernard's words as he left. Did the whole church think of Alice as James' friend – should this be a concern? And what of Alice's renowned ability for getting at the truth? James still had several months ahead of hiding the truth from everyone. Should he stop talking to Alice? He dismissed this possibility out of hand, telling himself that Alice would definitely suspect something if he started avoiding her. More importantly, he really enjoyed seeing her.

His thoughts were interrupted by the beep of a text arriving. It was from Alice and it immediately put James' own worries into perspective. Alice's mother had had a stroke and was in the local hospital. James replied, "On my way."

Facilities for visitors in the local hospital had improved a lot over recent years, as they had in many hospitals, and James was able to buy good quality coffee for himself and Alice. After a night at her mother's bedside, Alice had had no time for makeup. Her eyes were half open, her black hair scraped back and her clothes crumpled.

"Mum had a stroke about 5 o'clock yesterday evening. Fortunately a neighbour was with her and called for an ambulance straight away. They don't know how bad it is and it's too early to talk about long term effects but she's not responding much at the moment."

"I am so sorry, Alice. I want to help you in any way I can," James said. He wanted to give her a hug. Would that be inappropriate? Would Bernard have his spies out? While he agonised, the moment passed. Alice stared straight ahead and James was not sure she'd even registered what he'd said.

"I've never thought about Mum not being around. She's always been there for me."

"Would you like me to stay here while you go home for some rest?" James asked.

"I don't really want to be on my own."

It was unusual for Alice to say something like this, James thought. It showed the extent of the shock. As far as he knew, Alice's mother had been in good health, so this had come completely out of the blue. Alice was a strong and independent person but there are times when everyone needs support. It occurred to James that this situation would be much more straightforward if he were not Alice's vicar. He would have hugged her and offered to take her back to her house to get a change of clothes, or even back to his house to get some breakfast. Perhaps he should just ring Bishop John and resign on the spot. That would make life simpler. He could then be totally honest with Alice and that would also, he realised, be a huge weight off his mind.

"I'm here for you," he managed.

The words didn't really do justice to his mental turmoil but James felt he saw the hint of a smile from Alice in response. She had finished her latte and she seemed to relax, so much so that she slumped to one side and promptly fell asleep with her head resting firmly on his shoulder. James tried to avoid tensing up. Alice was clearly in desperate need of rest and James was happy to support her. On the other hand he felt that recently his life had been far less under his control than he was used to. A few months ago he would not have anticipated any of these events. Why couldn't things just run smoothly? He had had a faith he was comfortable with and a job he liked. His life was calm and full of positive things. Now it felt like he had been caught up in a negative cycle. He was almost expecting something bad to happen. What would it be? Maybe Bernard would walk in, followed by all the members of the Parochial Church Council. They would see their vicar with Alice asleep on him and Bernard would say, "This is totally inappropriate behaviour. Full stop."

James decided he was getting a bit self-obsessed. Here was Alice who had just had the shock of her life and could face months of emotional and practical challenges, and yet James was allowing himself to wallow in the comfort of self-pity. He thought about the difficult times ahead for Alice. The health of her mother would be the priority. Prospects for stroke survivors varied hugely, so there were currently many unknowns. However, Alice was self-employed. She had deadlines for her writing, and if she didn't write anything, she would not get paid. If he were not a vicar, James could suggest that Alice rented out her flat and moved in..... he stopped himself before this thought ran away with him.

"Yo, Vic!" Jack interrupted James' thoughts.

"Oh, hello, Jack," James managed, wondering whether being spotted by this fifteen-year-old tearaway could actually be worse than a visit from Bernard and the PCC.

"Are you all right?" Jack actually sounded concerned.

"Yes, I'm fine, thank you, Jack. I'm just here with Alice. Her mother is not very well."

"Stroke?"

"Yes, that's right. How did you know?"

"My nan died here," Jack explained.

"Oh, I'm sorry."

"Yeah, it wasn't good. Shit happens."

James could not disagree. Jack clearly wasn't quite ready to leave the two of them in peace.

"I suppose it helps if you don't think death is the end," Jack continued. "Then you have some hope and you don't get so desperate and sad."

51

"Even when you have hope, you can still get sad. It's okay to be sad, even years after you have lost someone."

"Yeah, I suppose you're right," Jack said and seemed to brighten a little. "Do you think being a vicar is about saying the right things?"

"I think that's part of it. So what are you doing in the hospital?"

"Me? Just a check-up."

"Is everything all right?" James asked.

"Yep, all fine," Jack replied quite quickly. "Is Alice okay?"

"Well, early days, but yes, I hope so."

"She looks like she's stayed up all night in those clothes," Jack said. "Still fit, though."

By the time James had considered whether or not to respond, Jack had moved on. 'Shit happens' and 'still fit' – James couldn't really argue with either of the statements that Jack had made. Perhaps, on reflection, a visit from Jack was preferable to one from Bernard and the PCC. What a strange thing for a vicar to conclude. As he started to think again about how he could best help Alice, James couldn't help notice that she was very quietly and very subtly starting to snore. James would never have believed it but now he knew - there was such a thing as cute snoring.

CHAPTER 9

The internet had changed people's lives for the better in so many ways. Advice sites and videos for all sorts of ailments have helped scores of worried surfers. However, information about serious and complicated conditions could sometimes do more harm than good. James was aware of this and his own search on the subject of strokes soon gave him the impression that there were about as many different types of stroke as there were sufferers. He knew Alice well enough to assume that she would spend hours researching the topic of strokes on as many apparently reliable websites as she could find (research was a significant part of her working life, after all). She would probably then read a few personal accounts or blogs written by stroke sufferers. All of which would do her no good whatsoever, James felt. She could end up either sick with worry or full of false hope. Nobody knew at present the course her mother's condition would take. Hence it was entirely logical for James to insist that Alice was on her own as little as possible. The hospital staff were still considering the best course of treatment and would keep Alice informed. James knew Alice was an only child. He was never sure about her father, though it was clear he was not around. There was little to be gained from staying at the hospital when Alice desperately needed sleep, and sleeping on a waiting room chair with a vicar's shoulder as a pillow was only a short term solution. The plan was for James to drive Alice back to her flat (where she promised to sleep) and then she would text once she woke up to decide on her next move. The hospital would have James' number too, in case Alice was in a deep sleep.

Having dropped Alice off at her flat and made her repeat the mantra "sleep not surf" three times (which at least raised a weak smile from her), James returned to his house, where Stan was again tending the garden.

"Time for a cup of tea, vicar?" Stan asked as James got out of his car.

"Of course, Stan. Great job as usual. I'll put the kettle on."

Though it was a predictable routine, James was actually quite pleased to see Stan. He was feeling quite unsettled and sometimes his tendency towards introversion needed to be kept in check. A bit of company would be welcome.

"A good evening last night," Stan said as they settled to the freshly brewed tea. "Mind you, you need to keep that Bernard in check. I think you could be a bit firmer with him sometimes."

"Maybe," said James, "but the whole point of the evening is to see that even within the same church, there will be differences over interpretation. But we can live with them. Those verses about love were very important."

"I expect you might need to bring them out again at the church Away Day. I'm sure some people will want to air their views, whatever the topic."

James had forgotten about his plan to have a church Away Day where the congregation had some social time together as well as looking at a Christian theme in detail. Maybe that could wait for the next vicar too.

"I tell you one thing Bernard can't live with," said Stan with a twinkle in his eye.

"What's that?" asked James.

"Being called Bernie! Spirited woman, that Barbara! I like a spirited woman. Do you like a spirited woman?"

James decided to change the subject.

"How did you get on at the new charity shop?"

"Ah, yes. Well, they said they'd let me know. Mind you, not sure I'd like to work there anyway. I walked in the door and could hardly move. I'd knocked three knick knacks off the shelves before I got to the till and then got my coat caught on one of the hangers that was sticking out. I told them they needed to rearrange the whole layout and stock some more modern stuff. There's no money in knick knacks."

James thought Stan would probably continue as his gardener for the foreseeable future.

"You're looking a bit tired, vicar," Stan noted.

"Yes, I didn't sleep too well last night. It was probably just winding down from the meeting."

"Well, I admire you for running one. When I was in charge of my company, the last thing I wanted was all and sundry having their say. You never knew where it would lead."

"Yes, but running a company is different. In a church you are all seeking the truth together. It's a sort of journey, and you never know what you might encounter on the way. So it's important to let people have their say."

"So will you have an evening on the role of women in the church? There'll be lots of people who want to have their say there!"

"Well, maybe next year," James replied.

James' phone rang to prevent the conversation going further. It was the hospital. They could not get a response from Alice and they were keen for her to come in. From the urgent tone of the caller, this did not sound good. James agreed to ensure Alice made it to the hospital as soon as possible. He made his excuses to Stan and drove over to pick up Alice.

"I think it is unlikely to be good news," Alice said as they made their way to the hospital. "It seems the first 24 hours are crucial. There must be something concerning them."

"You've been googling, haven't you?"

"I'm afraid it's what I do. Just for twenty minutes and then I fell asleep," Alice admitted.

"I knew you would and it's not always helpful. I nearly rang your service provider to tell them to cut you off."

"Really?"

"No, not really. You'd probably have found a way round it anyway."

At the hospital they made their way to the stroke ward and were invited by a doctor into her office. Alice and James shared a quick worried glance as they entered.

"I'm afraid we were not able to do any more for your mother. She never regained consciousness and she died a little while ago. I'm so sorry," the doctor said.

She may have said it many times before but she sounded genuine.

She paused to let her words sink in before asking gently, "Would you like to see your mother?"

"No," Alice replied quickly. "No, I want to remember her as she was. Thank you."

"Would you like some time on your own?" the doctor asked.

Alice nodded and the doctor left.

James and Alice sat alone in silence for several minutes. Finally Alice spoke.

"I hope she didn't suffer at the end."

James thought of several things to say but they all sounded so trite he ended up saying nothing. He listened as Alice continued.

"She had a faith and I believe she is now with God.... I don't really know how that works.... but I know that it has to be good.... this is the ultimate test of faith, isn't it?"

James could still not think of anything he wanted to say.

"Thank you for being with me, James."

CHAPTER 10

In the café a week later Alice looked as though she had at least had some sleep. James bought the coffees and they sat together in silence for a while. Alice finally spoke.

"They say that work can be a blessing in these situations. It gives you something to focus on and reduces the risk of wallowing and reflection. The past week has been intense. I've cried, I've raged at God, I've never felt so exhausted. And I've thought about Mum virtually all the time."

James nodded.

"I feel like I want to start some work but I've also got this feeling that I'm letting Mum down if I think about anything else."

"I don't think you are," James said gently.

"Hmm. You're quite good at knowing when to speak and when not to speak."

"Thank you."

"Was it part of your training?"

James smiled. Was it too soon for flippancy?

"Yes, Wednesday afternoons with Bishop Hugh."

Alice smiled.

"Tell me about them."

"The only ones I remember are - if you notice the congregation asleep during the sermon, don't say anything. If you notice the organist asleep, best to say something."

Alice smiled again. "Not your best joke, but I appreciate the effort."

"What sort of cars do vicars like?" James asked.

"Is this a better joke?"

"Convertibles."

"That's terrible," Alice said. "You obviously didn't go to Bishop Hugh's sessions on jokes for vicars."

"How rude!" said James, in mock offence.

"I really would like to do that article on the working week of a church minister," Alice went on. "I just feel at the moment I need plenty to be working on and I'm pretty sure I could sell it."

James felt trapped. After what Alice had been through, he could not possibly knock her back.

"Okay. Journalistic persistency versus ecclesiastical reluctance – I don't really stand a chance!"

"Interesting way to put it. Can I quote that?" Alice asked.

"Whoa, slow down. I think we would need some ground rules."

"What sort of ground rules?"

"I don't know yet," James played for time. "Maybe we'll start with - the journalist buys the coffees."

Alice got up with a smile. James sighed inwardly as he realised he was on very dangerous ground. Yet his feelings were mixed. The thought of regular meetings in his dairy with Alice cheered him up. At the same time he realised there would be difficult moments when he might just give away how he was really feeling about his faith.

He could try to limit the discussion to details of his routine, but that would make for a very boring article. Alice was the last person in the world he wanted to lie to. In fact he would love to open up to her.

"Hello! I'm back!"

James realised Alice was trying to get his attention; he had obviously not noticed that she had returned with the coffees.

"That's the second time recently you've been deep in your own world. Is everything all right?" Alice asked.

"Yes, yes," James replied quickly. "I was, er, I was just trying to remember some more of Bishop Hugh's jokes. His wife was on the stage, you know."

"Really?" Alice smiled. "I think I can see a punchline coming."

"You can?"

"It's likely to involve the words 'As the actress said to the Bishop'. I think Bishop Hugh needs to stick to theology - or maybe you do."

They sipped their coffees in comfortable silence.

CHAPTER 11

As James approached his house, he noticed a figure on the doorstep. This was not unusual as he had regular visits from people in the congregation and even, in the case of Simon, from other congregations. However, he didn't immediately recognise the stocky figure leaning against the porch. He had a familiar look about him and as James got nearer, he gradually realised who it was. Apart from smug Christmas letters and oversized birthday cards, James had not heard from him in several years – and he hadn't actually seen him for longer than that. It was his brother, Peter.

"Hey, James! How's my little brother? Great to see you! You're looking so well – this vicaring life obviously suits you."

"I'm well, thanks, Peter. This is a surprise. Do you want to come in for a cup of tea?"

"That would be great. It's what you do with vicars, isn't it?"

As Peter turned to enter the house, James noticed he had a small suitcase with him. James made some tea, found some Rich Tea biscuits and sat down with Peter.

"Do you know, if I had to guess what biscuits a vicar would serve with tea, I would have guessed these!" Peter said, tucking into his second. "Very nice, too!"

"Are you in the area on business?" James asked. He couldn't imagine that Peter was simply feeling guilty that he had not seen his little brother in years and wanted to see how he was.

"To be honest, James, I was feeling a bit guilty I hadn't seen my little brother in years and I just wanted to see how you are."

"Hmm," said James. "And you're hoping to stay."

"Well, that's very kind of you."

"You've brought a suitcase."

"Ah yes," Peter said, looking down as if seeing the case for the first time. "Well, I always like to be prepared for all possibilities. You know, my work takes me all over the country and I never know when I might have to stay on a bit longer."

"So you're doing some work in the area?" James asked.

"Well, I might do. You know me, I'm always looking for business opportunities and this area is quite well off...."

"You're being very vague, Peter. You're beginning to worry me."

"There's nothing to worry about, James! You always were a bit of a sensitive one, weren't you, what with your pretend friend in the sky and everything. No, it's nothing to worry about. I just need a change of scenery for a bit – just while a deal is going through."

"So you've upset somebody?" James asked.

"James, that is part of business! There are always winners and losers, and the losers get upset. It's only natural. But it's probably best if I just have a bit of a break while this latest bit of business settles down."

"So no one knows you're here."

"Who is there to tell? You know me, I don't like ties, not ready for settling down, and I'm often travelling on business. So the only other person who knows I'm here is you! And God, if you want to count Him."

James knew Peter was inclined to bend the truth and his mocking attitude towards faith grated on him, but he was his brother. He could hardly turn him away, even though he suspected there was far more to Peter's situation than he was letting on. Peter also had the gift of the gab and a salesman's charm; having him around for a few days might take his mind off his own problems. As James was considering how to respond, there was a knock at the door.

It was Stan, ready to work on the garden. James greeted him.

"Hello, Stan, good to see you. All well with you?"

"Yes, fine thanks, vicar. Oh, sorry, I see you've got company."

"Yes, this is....."

However, before James could introduce his brother, Peter had barged past him to shake Stan's hand and introduce himself.

"Pleased to meet you. I'm Jeremy. I was at college with James. I'm working in the area so I thought I'd catch up with my old friend."

James stared at his brother.

"Well, that's nice," Stan responded. "I'm Stan. I help James out with his garden. Well, I'm sure you two must have a lot of catching up to do, so I'll leave you to it."

Peter shut the door as Stan turned away. James continued to stare at him.

"You'd better tell me what's going on," James said.

CHAPTER 12

Standing in the kitchen opposite Peter, James was suddenly seething. He had always felt naïve in comparison to his brother, and now he had the distinct feeling he was being taken for a ride by his worldy-wise sibling.

"What the bloody hell is going on?" James demanded.

"Ooh! Sweary vicar!"

"Don't hide behind sarcasm, just tell me the truth!"

Peter took a moment to think.

"Yes, I'm sorry. I do owe you an explanation."

"You're pretending to be someone called Jeremy. And you're presumably expecting me to back up your lies. This had better be good!"

James was not calming down.

"I'm in a little difficulty," Peter started.

"You mean you've upset someone in a big way."

"People get upset in business all the time," Peter said with a half-smile.

"And do people pretend to be someone else all the time? Or is that only when they're in deep trouble?"

"I'm not in deep trouble."

"That doesn't sound convincing."

"Look, I just need to take a break from the intense world of business dealings for a while. You must have parishioners who suffer from work-related stress. Think of me as one of them," Peter said.

"They don't tend to change their name to Jeremy. And they are nearly always open and honest with me."

"I am being honest with you. I do need to take a break," Peter continued.

"How dodgy is this business you're involved in?"

"Well, that's not very Christian, accusing your own brother of dodgy dealings. Look, I stand to make a lot of money which means someone else will lose out on some money."

"They're not happy so you're keeping out the way."

"As I say, these things happen all the time in my line of business. But, yes, that's part of it," Peter conceded.

"Part of it?"

"Yes, I mean, that's essentially it. Things will all blow over in a few days."

"I'm worried you said 'part of it'."

"I may have been sleeping with his wife."

"Look, Peter. You've got yourself into this mess, you've got to live with it. Don't involve me."

James picked up Peter's suitcase and walked to the front door.

"Hang on James," Peter pleaded. "I am sorting it out. I just need somewhere away from home for a couple of nights. I don't want to involve Mum and Dad."

James hated these situations. He wasn't close to his brother and he knew he couldn't be trusted – but he had told him the mess he was in. If he marched out with his suitcase, Stan would be sure to notice. In fact he wouldn't be surprised if Stan was weeding very close to the front door to try to eavesdrop on their conversation. Did he really want Stan (and the rest of the church) to know about this aspect of his family affairs?

"Nice one, Peter. You knew the threat of worrying Mum sick would be a strong card."

"I didn't mean it like that…" Peter started to protest.

James dropped the suitcase.

"You can stay tonight but no longer."

CHAPTER 13

James didn't know which church or minister had first come up with the idea of a Church Away Day. Maybe it was a very lively Anglican church back in the seventies. Or perhaps it had come from America – one of those enormous congregations where it's easy to get lost in the crowd. He could see the logic in the idea of an Away Day. Churchgoers tended to meet briefly on a Sunday. Some would attend a midweek meeting, but there was never any extended time together where you got to know each other well and found out what people were really thinking. It was a great idea in theory but at this particular point in his life, it was the last thing James needed.

As Stan, Barbara and Bernard arrived for the planning meeting, James was struggling to focus on the task in hand. He would much rather be spending time with Alice, supporting her as she worked through her bereavement. He also needed to give some thought to the situation with his brother. Just how much was Peter still keeping from him? The situation was obviously quite serious and James could imagine his brother getting involved in something criminal if it made him money. Things were likely to be much worse than Peter was admitting.

"I think we should look at what the Bible says a church should be."

Bernard's bold assertion brought James back to the present.

"What do you mean, Bernard?" James managed.

"Well, are we the sort of church that we should be? What does the Bible say about what we should be like as a church?"

"Look, Bernard," Barbara interrupted, "if you want the day to be about the role of women in church, then just say it!"

"I'm not just talking about women," Bernard said. "It's much broader than that. There's a whole range of guidance about how a church should operate. I think we should look at the whole picture."

"No doubt the role of women in leadership will come up," Barbara countered. "You think women should sit quietly in church, probably with some sort of head covering, whereas I can see Jesus spending time with women and taking them seriously in what was a very patriarchal society. We're never going to agree on this."

James decided to step in.

"Yes, I think the idea of a church Away Day is to build up the church...."

"Not to allow healthy debate?" Bernard objected.

"Healthy debate is good but there are certain issues – secondary issues in my view – where people have their views and they'll probably not change. And it doesn't matter too much that there are different views within the church. The fact that we can live together and respect each other is the important thing."

"How about the nature of truth as a theme for the Away Day?" Stan suggested. "Nowadays it's all a bit wishy washy – you know, if it's true for you then that's fine, different things can be true for different people. The idea of absolute truth is going out of fashion."

James felt uncomfortable with the idea of focussing on truth when he was having to avoid it more and more in his life. The thought of leading a session on the nature of truth would have been fine until a few weeks ago. Now he was not sure he could actually get through it. He thought again about his brother. Peter was such a comfortable liar. Maybe James could pick up some tips and just sail through the day deceiving people.

"What do you think, James?" Stan was looking to him for a response.

Before James could answer, Barbara made a suggestion.

"I heard someone on the local radio – you know, the religious slot – talking about that. It was very interesting. I'd love to hear more from him. Maybe we could see if he's available. He's probably a local church leader."

James could have hugged her. The idea of an outside speaker was perfect for the situation he found himself in. He tried not to sound too excited.

"I think a speaker from somewhere else could work very well. Everyone is used to listening to me, week in and week out. A different perspective, a different style could fit the bill perfectly. It would make the Away Day different from Sunday church."

"That's not a bad idea, actually," agreed Stan. "And, to be honest, you've seemed a bit hassled recently so it would give you a break."

James was worried that Stan was noticing a difference, but also delighted that he could avoid having to prepare talks on truth when he was living a lie. Rather predictably Bernard was ready to throw a spanner in the works.

"We'd have to make sure he's sound."

"You mean ask him about his views on women?" Barbara said.

"I'm sure we can check up on him, Bernard," James added quickly. "If you let me have the details, Barbara, I'll see what I can find out."

CHAPTER 14

"So, ground rules," said Alice.

James was enjoying the coffee and Alice's company. Could they not just sit quietly together? Why spoil it with awkward questions? He decided to play for time.

"Well, what are your normal ground rules?"

"Not a lot really. Sometimes I have to make it clear I'm not going to sleep with the guy I'm interviewing…"

"Really?"

"Yes, you sound shocked. I'm talking certain types of male here. Not vicars."

"No. Well, you haven't interviewed a vicar before."

"Or were you shocked that someone might want to sleep with me?" Alice was almost looking offended.

"No!"

People at the other tables in the café looked round at them. That had obviously been louder than James intended. They had hardly started and this was already getting embarrassing. Alice also looked a little unsure of what was going on.

"Apart from that, I just ask questions and if they really don't want to answer, they say so – or they tell lies."

"Okay. So, can you tell when someone is lying?"

"Often."

"And what do you do then?"

"I stop buying the coffees."

"There's no messing with you."

Alice smiled, then looked more serious.

"Actually I usually call them out."

James didn't know what to say. Why was his life suddenly so complicated? If he went back on his agreement about the article, it would be unfair on Alice and also look rather obvious that he had something to hide. Alice would probably write an article about dishonest people, focussing mainly on a young vicar who had lost his way.

"So, what aspects of a vicar's life are you hoping to include in the article?"

"I think your daily routine would be quite interesting. Most people go to an office, get stuff done and go home. Is that what you do? Do you plan in advance what you're doing every day? What if someone in the church is in great difficulty? Do you say, sorry I'm planning my sermon?"

"Okay. We can talk about that sort of thing."

"For example, when you came to be with me at the hospital, did you have to rearrange a load of stuff or does your week have some inbuilt bereavement flexibility?"

"IBF"

"Sorry?"

"Inbuilt bereavement flexibility."

"Oh, another of Bishop Hugh's jokes?"

"Yes, sorry, not one of his best."

"I did appreciate your time and support then. I hope you know that," Alice said.

"I do. I'm pleased I was there for you."

"I still can't believe she's gone. I expect to see her at any moment. I guess that's normal."

"I think it is."

They took a moment to sip their coffee and reflect.

"Do you want to take more time off?" James asked.

"Oh no. Work definitely helps. It's a bit of normality I need at the moment."

James was pleased but he braced himself for more challenging questions.

"I think what people would be more interested in is your sense of calling," Alice continued. "The idea that you feel you were meant to do this job. Let's face it, there is some cynicism out there about church leaders. It's not been helped by paedophile scandals, and then there's the view that church ministers enjoy a low-key comfortable life in return for delivering an old-fashioned ritual on a Sunday – with a nice house thrown in."

"This is not sounding good."

"Believe me, I want this to be positive. I'm hoping to show that a church minister has a vital role in the community, reminding us of eternal truths when we're just running round chasing our petty ambitions and looking out for number one."

"That's a good way of putting it," James agreed. "I think your article's nearly written."

"No, no, it's a long way off. To make it convincing we need to get a real insight into a church minister's sense of his own role – the theory needs to be grounded in a real person."

"And I'm that real person."

"You don't miss much, do you, vicar?"

In spite of his serious misgivings about the interview, the awkward questions he would face and the very real risk that she would call him out, James had to admit he loved the time he spent with Alice.

CHAPTER 15

Having made some progress with the Church Away Day (and of course enjoyed his chat with Alice), James was in a relatively positive mood as he drove back home. Then he remembered Peter would be there – or Jeremy as he was calling himself – or dishonest, untrustworthy, possibly criminal Jeremy, to give him his full title. James could feel his mood worsen and his shoulders tense as he thought about what he should say to his brother. He'd told him he could stay for just the one night, so he should be packing his bags ready to leave. James doubted that would be the case. Was he ready for a confrontation? Would Peter really go to their parents? That would be very unfair on them and James did not want to play a role in forcing that.

As he entered the house, he discovered that his brother was not alone.

"Hello, Simon," James said, as positively as he could.

"Good morning, Reverend Chambers," Simon replied, earnest as ever. "I called round hoping to talk further with you about guidance but you were not available. Consequently I have been talking to Jeremy and he has been telling me about all the different roles that there are in business."

"Has he, indeed?" James looked at his brother with suspicion.

"I'm just wondering whether this is one of those chance situations where I am finding guidance in an unexpected place."

"I'm thinking it probably isn't," James replied as calmly as he could, wondering what sort of role Peter was planning for Simon in sorting out the mess he was in. "In fact it definitely isn't. I think the sort of business Jeremy's involved in wouldn't sit easily with the values of a Christian."

"Oh, Jeremy talked about how businesses make the world a better place. It sounds very positive and he thought he could see me playing a part."

85

James was beginning to get angry. He needed to end this conversation before he said something he shouldn't.

"Haven't you got some packing to do?" he asked his brother.

"Of course, yes, I'll get on."

Peter went upstairs, leaving James to seethe and Simon a little mystified. Simon seemed to be one of those people who coped with silences and was unable to sense the awkwardness of a situation. Whilst others might realise it was time to leave, he simply stood waiting. James took his time too, realising he needed to calm down and then try to support Simon, who had after all come round to talk further with him. Their last conversation had obviously been useful enough for him to want more.

"How did you get on with your IKEA application?" James eventually asked.

"Oh, I decided not to pursue that. I am considering another possibility, which explains my visit to see you. I would very much like to talk to you about being a church minister."

Fortunately James had perfected the art of not giving away too much with his facial expression, though a skilled body language reader might have detected his desire to scream. Why couldn't people leave him alone? It was one thing talking to Alice about his work but the thought of answering Simon's intense questions for any length of time would drive him over the edge. As he often did when unsure what to say, James asked a question.

"What did you want to know about the role?"

"It is a very public role on a Sunday but it is not clear what you do the rest of the week. It would be very interesting to do some work shadowing. I have been advised that work shadowing can give a valuable insight into a particular role and can help to clarify career goals."

Could the day get any worse? The prospect of Simon following him around filled him with thoughts that were very much at odds with the values of a Christian. Maybe he should call his brother down and let him carry on with his recruitment chat.

"People often talk to me in confidence," James explained. "There are many situations where I couldn't allow a young man to be work shadowing. And then there are solitary activities, like writing a sermon – that would be very dull to watch."

Simon was not put off.

"Oh, I realise it would not be appropriate in every situation but I am thinking there must be something during your working week where I could be present without having a limiting effect on what you do."

"Let me have a think about it, Simon," James said, hoping to draw the conversation to a close.

"I do appreciate that, Reverend Chambers," said Simon. "I would not wish to get in the way and I hope I might actually be useful to you."

When James said he had things to do, Simon finally left. James felt drained. There was just too much going on and he was having to be so careful about what he said.

"I can't get through to Mum and Dad."

Peter had appeared at the bottom of the stairs.

"So, you're really going to land them with your problems?"

Peter nodded.

"I've got no choice, have I?"

"You've got plenty of choices, Peter. And you've made some very bad ones. I don't want Mum and Dad affected by this."

"So, I can stay?"

"One more night."

They both knew Peter would be staying longer than that.

CHAPTER 16

"So, I've found out a bit about John Turner. You'll be pleased to know he's very sound. He's in charge of an Anglican church where the preaching is Bible-based and he's available for our Church Away Day. So, well done to Barbara for suggesting him."

James was pleased the Away Day planning group was making progress, and particularly pleased that Barbara, Stan and Bernard were all willing to take responsibility and put the work in to make things happen. Once he'd contacted John Turner, James had been happy to allow Barbara to liaise further with him to make a draft plan for the day. She reported on the progress they had made.

"We agreed the title for the day would be Truth in an age of Relativism….."

"That could be a bit off-putting, don't you think?" Bernard interrupted. "It sounds a bit academic. We're not all university buffs, you know. Can't we just go with 'What is Truth?' Or 'Truth in the 21st Century'?"

James found it difficult to know with Bernard whether he was just disagreeing with Barbara because he didn't get on with her, or whether he had a valid point. Bearing in mind the range of people in the congregation likely to attend the Away Day, James thought Bernard's idea was worth considering on this occasion.

"Some people may be more likely to come with a simpler title," James conceded. "I think 'Truth in the 21st Century' might do the trick. Let's go with that for now."

Barbara looked a little miffed.

"We'll call it a working title," she said.

"Yes, that's the working title and we'll carry on pondering while we do the planning," James suggested.

"Okay, I'll let John know," Barbara agreed, making a note. "As far as the plan for the day is concerned, he is very flexible, so he's happy to change things but at the moment we're thinking of an interview to start off with."

"An interview?" James queried.

"Yes, something fairly light, not theological as such, but just to show the importance of truth in human interactions. How things start to fall apart if people don't care about the truth."

James was beginning to feel uncomfortable. It worried him how often he had this feeling nowadays. It was almost as if everyone knew he was living a lie and they were gradually closing in on him.

"Right. So that will need some planning. Who was he thinking of interviewing?"

"We thought you would be good, James."

James sighed inwardly. He worked hard to push away mental images of the whole congregation slowly walking towards him with a lie detector.

"I don't know," he countered. "People know I will just give the right answers. And I was hoping the day would not be too much about me. Maybe it would be more interesting to have someone who could talk about truth from a different setting. Maybe from a workplace perspective."

"I could do it," suggested Stan. "I've seen all sorts in my business dealings. Avoiding the truth often leads to problems. People think everyone lies all the time in business and gets away with it, but I've got lots of stories about the truth being important. To be honest, I could probably tell my younger self a few things. Maybe I could have avoided some of the rough times I went through."

"You seem to have ended up all right," said Bernard. "You don't need to work again, do you?"

"True I'm okay financially, but there's a few things I'd have done differently."

"We want to keep it quite light," said Barbara. "We're not planning a confessional."

"Don't worry," Stan said. "I'll hit the right note."

Letting Stan loose was slightly risky but James thought it was a much better option than doing it himself.

"Let's go with Stan, then," James suggested and to his relief no one objected.

"What about the rest of the day?" Bernard asked. "We don't want to listen to Stan telling us about his business dealings for too long. You can get that over coffee every Sunday morning."

Bernard seemed to thrive on being blunt and provocative. Fortunately Stan knew Bernard well and was rarely upset by him.

"Actually, I think you'll find I'm often discussing more important stuff – like what we heard in the sermon."

"Really?" said Bernard. "I don't remember you ever talking to me about anything like that."

"I wonder why that is," countered Stan.

"Okay, let's think about the plan for the rest of the Away Day."

James felt it was time to get the meeting back on track. "Did you discuss anything with John, Barbara?"

"Just in broad terms. We're thinking he will look at Bible passages which relate to the importance of truth and give a short talk on each one, followed by some discussions in small groups."

"How will we arrange the small groups?" Bernard asked.

James knew this was a tricky area. There were certain combinations of people which could lead to challenging interactions. Those combinations usually involved Bernard.

"If I'm with some wishy-washy liberals, I'll be telling them what's what," Bernard added, confirming James' fears.

"Maybe Bernard could be in a group of one," Stan suggested, taking the opportunity to get back at Bernard.

Barbara looked at James with some sympathy.

"I'll be having a think about the groups," James said. "I think either John or I will need to say something about respecting other views too."

"Another passage about loving each other, I'll bet," said Bernard.

"It's all in there, Bernard," James responded. "Love one another is a common phrase in the New Testament."

"Yes, well, you may know your Bible. What I know is what people are like …."

After the initial relief of avoiding a major role in the Away Day, James was back to regretting the whole venture. Short of pulling off a disappearing act like his brother, James could not think of any other escape route. If only he had someone he trusted and respected to discuss it with.

CHAPTER 17

Approaching his favourite coffee shop, James was trying to work out which feeling was stronger, his desire to spend time with Alice or his anxiety at trying to hide the truth from her. He reached his conclusion as he opened the door – being with her trumped everything else. As he walked past the counter to their usual table, he was taken aback to see that Alice was not alone. In the crowded space, he could not immediately work out who she was talking to. James was surprised at the negative feelings he was experiencing, taking time to process them. There was certainly jealousy, mixed in with the resentment that his time with Alice could be spoilt.

As he got nearer to the table, Alice looked up and smiled, and James realised it was Jack who was sitting opposite her. He wondered what was going on – he didn't think they knew each other.

"Yo, Vic!" Jack greeted him, standing up as he did so. "Just keeping your seat warm."

James hadn't seen Jack since they had been at the hospital.

"Everything all right, Jack?"

"Yeah, great. Better than being in a maths lesson…"

"I mean after your hospital visit." James remembered Jack had mentioned a check-up he was having.

"Oh, that, yeah. All fine. Everything's clear."

"That's good news. I'm pleased, Jack."

"Yeah, we were just talking about you, saying how easy it is to talk to you. I can actually say anything I want – not like teachers – I can say what I really think and you don't seem to judge."

"There is a difference, Jack. The teachers are trying to get you to do something, like maths – I can just have a chat with you."

"Yeah, it's not a bad job you've got, is it? Just going round having a chat. I suppose you've got your Sunday stuff as well."

James was trying to think of a way to round off the conversation. Fortunately Jack decided it was time to leave.

"Anyway, see you again – hope it won't be a hospital corridor next time. Oh and Vic, don't forget to tell her you fancy her. Life's too short, mate!"

James watched as Jack left. He didn't dare to look at Alice. In fact he didn't know what to do.

"Hello, James."

He realised he hadn't actually acknowledged Alice as yet.

"Sorry, Alice. How very rude."

"Jack?" Alice asked.

"No, me. I haven't even said hello. Would you like another coffee?"

"No, I'm fine – and I've already got you one."

James sat down and wondered where to start.

"I didn't realise you knew Jack," he said.

"I don't really. He introduced himself and then just started chatting. He's very articulate. Worldly-wise but presumably heading for no qualifications."

"Yes, I don't know what's gone wrong with him. He's never been able to stay at any school. I think he's quite clever but he just can't accept authority."

"He'll probably start his own business one day and make millions."

"Probably. So, how have you been?" James asked.

"Not great at times. But I've been keeping busy. Having work to do definitely helps."

"What have you been working on?"

Alice explained that she had been planning the article about James, drawing up a list of areas to talk about so that she had plenty of information to bring together in order to create the final piece. There were areas where James would be happy to answer fully and without hesitation, such as his routine, the nature of his training, his line manager, whether he had any performance management in place. Other areas would involve James thinking carefully about what to say. Alice had included 'periods of doubt' in her list, which James was not looking forward to. He had read up online about how to tell if someone was lying and found that looking to the left could supposedly be a sign. James knew he would not be a good liar (he hadn't had a lot of practice, after all) and was wondering whether he ought to look to the left every time he answered a question, then Alice would think it was just a habit and nothing to do with avoiding the truth.

"What do you think?" asked Alice.

"It's a full and thorough list. I wouldn't have expected anything less."

"Thank you."

"What about confidentiality?"

"Where would it come up?"

"What if we're talking about the challenge of dealing with awkward members of the congregation? Even if you changed the names, local people would know who it was. Someone like Bernard has his awkward moments," James explained.

"Nicely understated. Bernard is awkward full stop."

They both smiled.

"Grammarians will tell you there is something called the Oxford comma. I'm hoping to get them to recognise the Bernard full stop," Alice continued.

"Ah, the Bernard full stop – used to indicate that the speaker is right and anyone who disagrees is unbelievably stupid."

"And should probably go to prison."

The discussion continued as they pondered the disappearance of the full stop in texting. Among some young people the full stop was seen as abrupt, almost rude. They got on to whether they checked their texts before sending – and if they did, was that a sign that they were officially no longer young.

As the waitress cleared their cups and asked if they would like anything else, they realised she was hinting that the café was closing soon.

"We've got no further with the article, have we?" Alice said.

"Ah well, I hear they open here every day and they've got plenty of coffee. Just let me know when you're free."

CHAPTER 18

Standing in the entrance hall having just arrived home, James looked down at the unsealed envelope full of 50 pound notes. Peter had handed it over and was smiling.

"You've certainly got some people who like you, James," he said. "Maybe I should have taken up this church business. Three grand bonus! Not bad, is it?"

"Three grand?"

"Yeah. I counted it. Couldn't resist – sorry. Still, your Stan's obviously got a fair bit of disposable income."

Peter explained that Stan had come round with a gift for James; some money for him to take a break. Stan had said he was worried James was looking particularly tired and under stress and thought he needed to recharge his batteries. In fact he couldn't remember the last time James had been on holiday. James couldn't stop himself wondering if it was too late to get a ticket to go and watch the England cricket team in the West Indies. A bit of sun and a couple of weeks just watching sport would do him the world of good. The thought was very attractive but could he really accept a gift like this?

"So, Stan reckons I'm heading for a breakdown?"

"Well, he didn't put it like that. He just said you were a bit stressed and could I pass this on to you," Peter explained.

"I can't possibly take it."

"Why ever not?"

"I'm just doing my job. There are times when it's challenging, like any job. It's not right to take huge gifts from parishioners."

"So you'd take a jar of home-made jam?"

Peter seemed ready for an argument.

"Well, yes, a jar of jam is different. This is three thousand pounds! That sort of money can make a big difference to a homeless charity or families struggling to get by."

"Sometimes you've got to think of yourself, James! We all need a break from work. You'll be no good to these people if you're running on empty all the time. And he has a point – you've got a lot on your plate at the moment."

James looked at his brother and they both knew what he was thinking – Peter was one of the main sources of stress for him. James realised he needed to take his time before deciding what to do with the cash. The thought of watching England bat at the Kensington Oval in Barbados was very attractive, particularly if it clashed with the Church Away Day. He'd always wanted to have a holiday watching Test cricket; this could be his one and only chance, particularly if he continued in his career as a church minister, although that was seeming less and less likely by the day.

"Would it be a convenient time to do some work shadowing?"

Simon had arrived and, seeing the door open, had just walked in. James quickly closed the envelope of cash.

"Good morning, Simon. How are you?" James asked to give himself time to think.

"I am physically very well, thank you Reverend Chambers. Spiritually I'm going through a searching time but I feel I need to test various options in order to see where I should be going."

"Did you think any more about those business roles I told you about?" Peter asked.

James knew he had to step in before his brother recruited Simon into something he would regret.

"Actually, Simon, I'm planning to visit a house-bound parishioner this week. Maybe today's the day. Anna doesn't go anywhere so we can call in any time."

"That would be great. Thank you, Reverend Chambers. Do I need to bring anything?"

"No, we can talk about her on the way. I think she would enjoy seeing someone new. Are you ready to go now?"

"Yes, absolutely. It will be interesting to see how a church minister operates in this situation."

James couldn't help thinking this was a mistake but Simon needed some support in finding his role in the working world. Maybe part of the process is ruling out jobs that he is clearly not cut out for. Anna was a sweet older woman and would cope with Simon. So that wouldn't be the problem. It was James who was struggling with Simon's earnestness. That holiday in Barbados was looking more attractive by the minute.

CHAPTER 19

On the way to visit Anna, James told Simon about her. She was a retired academic who was struggling physically. Unable to support herself in her own home, Anna had been keen to move in with one of her children. Unfortunately her children had other ideas and moved her into a nursing home. She was not unhappy but lacked the stimulation that she was used to, as many of the other residents had slowed down mentally as well as physically. James and Anna sometimes worked on crosswords together, as well as discussing current affairs.

"Do you like crosswords?" James asked Simon.

"I am very keen on general knowledge puzzles as I retain facts well."

"Anna likes cryptic crosswords."

"I have never understood cryptic crosswords."

James wondered whether he should just let Simon sit in silence while they were with Anna. They could then come to the obvious conclusion that church ministry was not for Simon. However, he knew Anna would not be happy to ignore a visitor and it would be interesting to see what she said about him.

"What do you like to do in your spare time, Simon?"

As James suspected, Anna was keen to engage with her new visitor.

"I am currently learning New Testament Greek," Simon replied.

"Why?"

Simon explained in some detail the advantages of knowing the original language of the Bible. He explained that Greek verbs not only have tenses but can also include aspect, which means that, in addition to being past, present or future, a verb can also be complete or incomplete. This verbal aspect is sometimes not clearly communicated in translation. So a knowledge of the Greek text can provide additional insights into the meaning of the New Testament.

"Really?" Anna seemed genuinely interested. "Can you give an example?"

Simon was not thrown by Anna's questioning. He quoted a verse from chapter five of Paul's letter to the Ephesians, "be filled with the Spirit." The aspect of the verb in Greek makes it clear that it means an ongoing process. It is not a one-off event. This aspect is not clear in the English translation.

"Very interesting," Anna said genuinely. "Do you go to a class to learn New Testament Greek?"

"No, it is an online course."

"And what do your friends think of it?"

"Friends?"

"Yes."

Simon seemed thrown by this question. James realised that Simon found grammatical nuances easier to understand than the concept of friendship, and his heart went out to him. At the same time he didn't know how he could help him. However, he felt he probably shouldn't be encouraging him to become a church minister.

"Do you fancy getting us some tea?" James suggested and Simon duly went off to the kitchen.

"Interesting young man," Anna commented, once Simon had left.

"Yes, he's a little bit lost in terms of what he wants to do in life."

"I'm sure he'll find his niche. He'll probably just stumble across it by accident and then feel more settled. And then perhaps relate better to other people. It's good of you to support him."

"Well, he wanted to see what's involved in the day to day life of a church minister."

"I think we all wonder that," Anna said with a smile. "You go from running a funeral service to solving cryptic cross word clues."

"It's got variety."

Anna looked down at her crossword.

" 'Seat of government initially found in beer' ".

"Hop. Surely you got that one straightaway. Houses of Parliament – initials Hop – hops are used to make beer."

"Of course. Just testing you."

Simon returned with the teas and sat in silence as James and Anna chatted. They each tried to involve him but things tended to peter out and he never took the initiative to ask a question or add a comment. It was clear that Simon had not yet found his niche.

CHAPTER 20

Sitting opposite Alice in the café was not quite delivering the sense of relaxation and escape that James hoped for. He realised he was feeling quite tense and Alice picked up on this too. Throwing caution to the wind, he decided to offload a little.

"Things are getting to me a bit at the moment. There are too many situations which are wearing me down and I can't really see them changing," he admitted.

"When you say situations, you really mean people," Alice suggested.

"Well, yes. Simon is well meaning but hard work, and the Away Day committee are also well meaning but they seem to like confrontation and scoring points off each other."

"I've been thinking about ways in which your role is different from other jobs, and this is the area where I think there's the biggest difference. Where can you let off steam when things aren't going well?"

"Yes, I have to be very careful. The Bishop tells me he's my safety valve."

"He's not exactly on the doorstep, is he? I suppose you could talk to your wife, if you had one."

James looked at Alice, unsure what to say. The notion of being able to tell her exactly what he thought and felt, every day when he finished work, was remarkably appealing. Was her question part of her journalistic research or was she suggesting something?

"Yes, that's true. But I haven't," James managed.

"Not yet."

"No."

"Do you think a single church minister does a better job than a married church minister?"

"No, not necessarily. Depends on the wife."

Their conversation was interrupted by someone approaching their table. James looked up to see his brother.

"Morning, James," he said. "What a lovely coffee shop."

Before James could respond, Peter then turned to Alice.

"Hi, I'm Jeremy. I was at college with James. I'm staying with him for a few days."

"Pleased to meet you. I'm Alice. You didn't tell me about Jeremy, James."

"No, I was trying to stick to business."

Alice explained that she was writing an article about James' working life and they met in the coffee shop for her to gather the information she needed. Much to James' disappointment, she invited his brother to join them. He readily accepted.

"So, are you a church minister too, Jeremy?" Alice asked.

"Oh no," Peter replied, as if it was the last thing he would do. "I work at GCHQ."

"Ah, so you're a linguist?"

"If I told you that, I would have to shoot you," Peter said with a smile. "All I can say is that GCHQ works hard to keep us all safe and I try to play my role within a very large organisation."

"Can you really not say any more than that?"

"I don't want to get into trouble, and I know what some journalists are like. I'm sure you're completely trustworthy, of course. Otherwise James wouldn't be working with you. But I do have to be very careful."

Alice turned to James whose mood had soured considerably. It was made worse by the fact that Alice seemed to be fascinated by his brother. James had to admit that Peter made a very good liar and his confidence and charm were impressing someone he thought of as very perceptive.

"Do you know any more about what Jeremy does?" Alice asked James.

James smiled. He couldn't help thinking of the forthcoming Away Day on Truth in the Twenty First Century. He was certainly not going to lie for his brother.

"I know quite a lot about him," he admitted, "but I think he'd probably shoot me if I told you."

"So you've managed to get him talking after a few drinks?"

"It's more what I've picked up over the years."

"Interesting," Alice said and looked at them both with an inquisitive gaze.

CHAPTER 21

Words from the Bible often popped into James' mind at unexpected moments. No doubt this was a consequence of years of studying the scriptures and delivering sermons. As he left the café, the list describing the fruit of God's Spirit went through his thoughts – love, joy, peace, patience, kindness, goodness, faithfulness, gentleness and self-control. In his grumpy and frustrated mood there was little sign of any of these. Perhaps it was time to see the Bishop again; the pretence and deception in his life were beginning to get to him.

James' thoughts were interrupted by a familiar voice.

"Penny for your thoughts, vicar," Stan said as James nearly bumped into him.

"Oh, hello, Stan. Sorry, I was miles away. How are you?"

"I'm fine, thanks. But I have to be honest, I'm a bit worried about you. You haven't been yourself for a while now. As if there's something on your mind."

James remembered the envelope with the money that his brother had passed on from Stan.

"Oh, Stan. Thank you so much for your generous gift! It's incredibly kind of you. That sort of money can make a big difference in someone's life."

"I don't want you giving it away now. That money is for you. I know when someone needs a break – I've seen it over the years in business. You give people a treat and they come back stronger and do a better job than ever. I think that's what you need at the moment. I don't know what's causing you so much stress and I daresay you can't let on, but I do know you need a break."

"Well, that really is very good of you, Stan," James said. "But three thousand is a lot of money...."

"Three thousand?" Stan interrupted. "I put five grand in that envelope."

James worked out instantly what had happened. He thought back to his brother handing him the envelope –

it had been opened. He was very tempted to tell Stan the truth but he resisted.

"Five thousand? Yes, I only had a quick look – and I'm not used to counting that amount of money. Don't worry, I'll check when I get home and let you know."

Stan looked uneasy but James did his best to reassure him and made his excuses. He headed straight home.

As he expected, there was only three thousand pounds in the envelope. James was angry at his brother for the deception and angry at himself for being so naive. As soon as Peter walked through the door, James confronted him. He knew his brother was one of those people who rarely experienced shame or guilt. He remembered reading about the personality traits of a narcissist. His brother possessed several of them – over confidence, risk-taking, lack of empathy, ability to move on from mistakes as if nothing had ever happened, little sense of guilt or shame. So it surprised James when his brother looked rather crestfallen.

"Yes, I took a couple of thousand," he admitted, avoiding James' gaze across the kitchen table. "I am in a bit of a tricky situation business-wise – nothing I can't handle, of course – but it seemed like too good an opportunity to miss."

"So you stole from your brother."

"Well, that's a very emotive way of putting it. I mean, it was a gift, and three grand is still a nice sum of money…"

"I want it back now."

James surprised himself at how firm he sounded. Peter looked at him, clearly weighing up his options. After a few moments he put his hand in his pocket and pulled out a wad of fifty-pound notes. James took the money and waited to see if his brother was going to apologise. The silence was finally broken by Peter.

"I have a lot of time for what you do here," he said, rather unconvincingly, "but my world is very different. I don't think you really have any idea how things work in my line of business. You have to operate by different rules otherwise you don't survive. You can't afford to think about right and wrong, you just have to get on with making things happen."

"So you just do whatever is necessary to make money."

"Yes, basically. And then you enjoy the benefits. You can't agonise about who might have fallen by the wayside. It's just the way it is."

James wondered again exactly what his brother was involved in. He was sure that most people in business would not recognise their working world from Peter's description. His brother was ticking more of the narcissist boxes with virtually every sentence.

"So would two thousand pounds solve your problems?" James asked.

Peter looked up at his brother with a half-smile.

"It would be a start," he said hopefully.

James shook his head and walked out.

CHAPTER 22

Sitting in his study, James had plenty to do. He needed to leave shortly for the next Away Day planning meeting so he wanted to be clear about the decisions still to be made and the jobs still to do. He also had a sermon to prepare for Sunday and had not even made a start on that. Yet he could not settle to either task as he wondered what to do about his brother. He found it very difficult to deal with someone so devious and dishonest. What was actually going on? How much did Peter owe? Had he actually done something illegal and was now on the run from the police? His thoughts were interrupted by the doorbell.

"Hi, James. So sorry to disturb you but I thought I might catch you both in."

"Both?"

James was a little thrown by seeing Alice on his doorstep. She had never called round before.

"Yes, you and Jeremy."

James invited her in, unsure what to expect, and they sat round the kitchen table. Peter had clearly moved on from any sense of letting his brother down and was his most charming self. Alice explained the reason for her unscheduled visit.

"This may be a complete non-starter but I was wondering about doing a piece on Jeremy. You see, I've never met anyone who works at GCHQ. Everyone's heard of it but not many people know what goes on. I think it could be really interesting. 'How Jeremy at GCHQ keeps us all safe' – something along those lines."

James was confident this would definitely be a non-starter. Firstly the man Alice was referring to was not really called Jeremy and secondly he didn't work at GCHQ.

"That sounds like a great idea!" Peter said.

James stared at Peter. How could he go along with this?

"I can see James is worried about the confidentiality aspect," Alice said, noticing James' reaction.

"He's a bit of a rule-keeper is James," Peter said with a smile. "You could always change my name in the article."

"Yes, what would you like to be called?"

James was really not enjoying Alice's playful tone and he was having trouble hiding his feelings.

"Maybe call him Peter," James said bitterly.

Peter moved on swiftly, the risk of being exposed barely registering with him.

"There are certain details I would have to leave out but I could talk in general terms about the sorts of things I do. Perhaps mention some foreign plots we have managed to foil. And then just bits about the day to day work. Much of it is surprisingly mundane."

"Would your boss be okay with it?" Alice asked.

"My boss?"

"At GCHQ."

"Oh, right, yes, I'd run it past him but I'm sure I could sell it to him. If you put in bits about how supportive he is, he'll go with it. He's a sucker for any sort of praise like that. We call him Butter Up Ben."

"Butter Up Ben?" Alice asked with a smile.

"Yes, that's not his real name of course. His real name's Geoff Farningham. Oh no! I've given away his identity. I'm going to have to shoot you now! James, can I borrow your gun?"

Alice smiled as Peter held his hand over his mouth in mock horror. However, James was not going to join in on the joke. He got up from the table. Peter leant over towards Alice and spoke in a mock conspiratorial tone.

"He's going to get his gun. He keeps it for parishioners who don't like his sermons."

"I've got to go now," James said flatly. "I've got a meeting about the Church Away Day – it's about the importance of truth. Good to see you, Alice. I'm sure Jeremy will let you out. Or should I call him Peter?"

As James shut his front door behind him, he realised he was actually quite looking forward to the planning meeting. The people there were honest and they were working towards a common goal. As he reflected on his brother's shameless behaviour and his own strong sense of resentment, James realised there was something else swirling around in the mix of unwelcome feelings. He had not liked the way Peter and Alice were interacting. He had rarely felt jealousy in his life, and this was not a good time for that most unpleasant of emotions to take a hold.

CHAPTER 23

"I just want to say how grateful I am for the time and effort you are giving to this Away Day. It really is above and beyond, and I appreciate your commitment to making sure it proves a worthwhile time for everyone."

James felt better for articulating his gratitude. He realised how good it was to deal with people who were genuine and, in Stan's case in particular, very supportive. He knew they had their differences and liked to provoke each other occasionally, but this was a breath of fresh air compared to his brother's unashamed and relentless dishonesty. Barbara, Bernard and Stan nodded politely and sat ready to get on with things.

"So we've sorted the speaker and the theme. Last time we were thinking about starting the day with an interview where Stan talks about the importance of truth."

"Yes, I've had a think about that," Stan said. "I've got a few stories about where truth was important in my career. Or dishonesty appearing easy and attractive but actually causing problems further down the line."

"That sounds good, Stan," James said.

"When you say 'a few stories', how long is this going to take?" Bernard asked, ready to take issue with Stan's proposal.

"Don't worry, Bernard. I can be concise and to the point. I used to hate meetings where people droned on so you won't catch me doing that."

"I'm wondering whether it would be better to have more than one interview so we get a perspective on truth in different situations," Bernard continued.

"So you'd like to be interviewed," said Stan, demonstrating his ability to be concise and to the point.

"Yes, I think it would be good. I have strong views on the value of truth and it wouldn't just be a few stories about business deals."

James thought about stepping in but decided to let them continue the debate. Bernard and Stan were very different but both seemed to cope with and almost enjoy the blunt exchanges they often had. Bernard had an administrative role with the local council which, James suspected, Stan did not regard as a proper job. It certainly lacked the cut and thrust of business and possibly explained why Bernard enjoyed a good argument in church circles. Barbara had not yet contributed to the meeting and James wondered what she was thinking.

"I think it would be interesting to have more than one interview but this part of the day is really just an introduction to the theme, rather than a statement of Biblical truth," James suggested. "I'm thinking perhaps five minutes per interview at most."

"Yes, I think we want people to focus on what John Turner says and also have plenty of time to look at what the Bible has to say," Barbara said. "I'm assuming anyone interviewed will basically say they got into difficulties by ignoring the truth or being dishonest, so it could get a bit samey and obvious."

"Stan and I are very different so I'm sure what we have to say would have some variety," Bernard replied.

The discussion continued as Stan and Bernard challenged each other about what exactly they would say and whose interview would be more interesting. James suggested Barbara might like to be interviewed but she turned down the opportunity. Eventually it was agreed that Stan and Bernard would send James the key points of their answers so that he could check they were sufficiently different and engaging to ensure a good start to the Away Day.

James felt they were making progress so he moved the meeting on to more practical issues. They agreed that they would pay for a caterer to deliver a main course for lunch and then ask for volunteers in the church to bring desserts, serve food and clear up. There was some discussion regarding quality control of the desserts that members of the congregation might bring, and Bernard even mentioned by name an older woman and the fact that she could give the whole congregation food poisoning. Fortunately Barbara knew the woman well and agreed to steer her towards a different role on the day. There was some discussion around drinks – would it be appropriate to serve alcohol?

"I'm reminded of the occasion where Jesus turned water into wine, thereby giving his blessing for our enjoyment of that fine drink," Bernard said.

"A large meal and a glass of wine at lunchtime tends to make me fall asleep," Barbara countered.

The others knew that Bernard enjoyed a glass of red but the group managed to agree it was best to avoid sluggish discussions in the afternoon. So for the sake of keeping people alert, it was noted that the drinks on offer would be tea, coffee and fruit juice. At the mention of discussion groups, Bernard asked whether James had organised these. James hadn't actually given it any thought but explained that he needed to know exactly who would be there on the day before making final decisions.

As James wound up the meeting, he felt pleased that they had made progress and particularly relieved that he was managing to avoid any significant role on the day. He thanked Barbara, Stan and Bernard for their contributions and they all got up to leave. James checked his phone as he went out the door and saw he had a text from Alice – 'Fancy a coffee?'

CHAPTER 24

Normally James would jump at the opportunity to see Alice but he hesitated before replying to her text. He needed to sort out what was going on. He knew what was happening on a factual level – Peter was telling a bunch of lies, turning on the charm and Alice could see an interesting article in the making. It was more a question of his feelings. Was he just annoyed that Peter was clearly enjoying the attentions of Alice when his actions actually deserved her complete disapproval? Was he jealous of the way Alice was entertained by Peter when that was James' role? On the other hand, what right did he have to be the only one to share jokes with Alice? He could tell her the truth about his brother. Would that put Peter in danger? And would that simply be motivated by jealousy? Perhaps things would become clearer when he actually sat down with Alice.

"See you in 30 mins," he replied.

"I'm worried about you," Alice said once they had sat down with their coffees.

"I'm worried too," James replied. "I've got a lot going on at the moment, what with the Away Day coming up, trying to support Simon and … well, lots of things."

"To be frank, that doesn't sound like a lot. I presume there are significant things you can't tell me about."

"I can't tell you about everything. You know that. There are confidentiality issues."

"I think you should go and see the Bishop."

James was taken aback. Did Alice think he ought to give up his job?

"We talked about him being a safety valve," Alice continued. "I think you might need one at the moment. I would happily offer but you've made it clear that wouldn't be appropriate."

"You make it sound like I'm heading for a breakdown!"

"You were very rude back there when I was talking to Jeremy. It's not like you. There's obviously something going on."

"I didn't like the way he let on about my having a gun."

"See – even your jokes aren't very good at the moment."

James sipped his coffee as he wondered how much more he could say. Alice asked if James was okay with her idea of an article about 'Jeremy'. She had googled his name and come up with nothing, which was very unusual for Alice as she was a dogged internet researcher. She wondered whether he had such an important role at GCHQ that they had somehow removed his digital presence. She was clearly fascinated by 'Jeremy' and talked about the sense of danger he emanated, as well as possessing an obvious charm and wit. James' coffee was tasting more bitter by the minute.

"Well, it's not up to me what you write your articles about," James managed to say. "I've known him for years and what I would say is that he's very good at just telling people what he wants them to know."

"Sounds like an ideal candidate for GCHQ," Alice said with a smile.

James got the impression that Alice had already made up her mind about the article and was just mentioning it to James out of politeness. He wondered whether this was the real reason she had wanted to see him, rather than to express her concern for his welfare. As if reading his thoughts, Alice changed the subject.

"I do think it would be a good idea for you to see the Bishop, though," she said. "He must have come across all sorts of situations with the vicars he manages. Is that the right word for what a Bishop does – 'manages'?"

"I expect there's a more ecclesiastical word. 'Oversees', perhaps."

"That sounds a bit like a supervisor. I think being a confidant or adviser or a holy support is what you need."

"A holy support? Sounds like worn out underpants."

"Your jokes aren't getting any better. So, you will go and see him then?"

James picked up his cup to give himself time to think before answering.

"Your cup's empty," Alice said. "I'll get you another if you like."

James shook his head. He really was feeling at a low point. Maybe it was time to call on his 'holy support.'

"Are you sure you want to carry on with the article?" Alice asked. "We can always shelve it and come back to it. If it's one less thing for you to think about, then maybe we should leave it for now."

"Oh no," James said. "I want to carry on."

Alice looked pleased. Though they led to some awkward moments, James realised that his meetings with Alice were still the highlight of his week. He wasn't going to let his brother spoil that. They looked at their diaries and agreed their next meeting.

CHAPTER 25

Having decided to spend a couple of hours putting together detailed plans for the Away Day, James was not best pleased to be interrupted by the doorbell. Simon had come round to discuss his work shadowing. He clearly felt it was worth continuing whilst James was sure it was a waste of time. Simon simply did not have the people skills required for a ministry role and seemed to be blissfully unaware of this. Rather than abandon his plans, James decided to continue with the task in hand whilst talking it through with Simon.

As they put together the schedule for the Away Day, Simon was surprisingly vocal. James was planning a handout for everyone which gave details of timings as well as Bible passages for the discussion groups to tackle. Once he had added the practical information of how lunch would be organised, where the toilets were and emergency procedures, the handout was looking quite crowded and unclear.

"The document is full of information but not in a user-friendly format," Simon said. "Shall I attempt to improve the layout?"

James was a little taken aback but decided to let Simon work on the document while he went to make some coffee. On his return, James was amazed at the transformation.

"That looks great, Simon," he said. "You've done a brilliant job!"

Simon did not immediately respond. He continued to stare at his work on the screen.

"It is a better version but there is potential to improve it still further. I wonder whether a folded sheet would be preferable. We would plan it A4 landscape and then fold it in the middle. The addition of some visuals would enhance the appearance too. Do you have any images in mind?"

James hadn't thought about it. He couldn't immediately think of any appropriate pictures.

"The day is about truth in the twenty-first century. There are no obvious pictures that go with that."

"Would you mind leaving it with me for a little while longer, Reverend Chambers?" Simon asked.

"No, that's fine," James replied, quite taken aback at Simon showing such initiative.

James wandered into the kitchen and picked up the newspaper. He turned to the sports pages and read a long piece on the dilemmas facing the England cricket selectors. They had too many wicket keepers and no world class spinners. He realised how little time he'd had recently to switch off from his role and take an interest in the outside world. Flicking through the rest of the paper, he noticed a report on the spread of the prosperity gospel in American churches. Using words from the Bible, preachers convince their congregation that God's plan for them is to live materially comfortable lives. The main point of the article was that the preachers were making a lot of money but this did not seem to deter their followers. James took a moment to reflect on how Bible verses can be used to promote all sorts of messages. Wrongly interpreted, the Bible can lead people into strange or bad choices. Of course there had always been arguments over interpretation - this was part of the reason why there were so many different types of Christian church – but it pained James to see the Bible being used for such apparently selfish ends. Enjoying a bit of time to himself, he was about to make a start on the crossword when Simon walked in.

"Would you like to come and consider what I have been working on, Reverend Chambers?" he asked.

James was very happy for Simon to talk through his work. He was impressed at the clarity of what he had produced. He had used a symbol at various points which looked like a set of weighing scales to suggest the idea of truth. The repeated image gave the document a corporate look. Overall, even to James' untrained eye, it felt like a professionally produced document.

"That looks great, Simon. Thank you!"

Simon nodded though he showed no emotion.

"Yes, I think it is quite effective. However, with more time I could make it clearer and more balanced," Simon explained.

"I think it's great as it is. People will think I've hired a designer. You really have a gift for this, Simon!"

As James looked at the screen, he realised that this was perhaps the type of work Simon should be considering. He clearly had an eye for what was visually effective and he was able to listen carefully to instructions. They looked together at websites which explained routes into graphic design and James finally felt he was making progress with Simon. Now he was starting to consider a career in design, the interest in shadowing James in his work should fall away. Things were certainly looking more positive, for both Simon and James.

CHAPTER 26

As Simon left, James noticed that Stan was working on the garden. This was surprising as he wasn't due for a few days. Perhaps Stan was at a very loose end and couldn't resist the good weather. James walked over to have a chat and find out more.

"Well, Stan, this is certainly going above and beyond," he said. "Not that I'm complaining, of course."

"I wanted to catch you actually," Stan explained. "I've been mulling things over. You remember I mentioned the envelope of money to you - did you check there was five grand in there?"

"Don't worry, Stan. I have got your full gift of five thousand pounds. And very generous it is too!"

"It's just there's something about your friend that I'm not sure about. When you mentioned three thousand, I got a feeling I hadn't had for years. The sense that someone had got the better of me. It didn't happen very often in my career but I remember each time very clearly. They were real low points."

"I can assure you I've got the full amount, Stan."

"It's a gut feeling about him. I don't know what it is, but you need to be careful."

"I appreciate your concern."

"Do you ever have gut feelings about people, good or bad?"

"Yes, I suppose I do. But I try to keep an open mind."

Stan accepted he might be wrong about James' guest, but he didn't sound convinced. They talked about the need to be worldly-wise and how easy it was for someone in James' position to be used. Church ministers tended to want to see the good in people and they talked about forgiveness but, in Stan's view at least, some people would take advantage of that, knowingly or otherwise.

James invited Stan in for a cup of tea and they continued their conversation. It was interesting to hear Stan talk about his life in business and James took the opportunity to ask a few questions that might help him to work out just how bad his brother's situation was.

"So I presume you upset a few people over the years?"

"Oh yes, that's part of the deal. You go into business knowing that it's a competition and there'll be winners and losers. You get upset when you lose and you tend to remember if someone has beaten you."

"And if you beat someone else, did you keep out of their way?"

"No, I didn't rub it in, but the people I dealt with tended to accept that you have to take some bad times. Your turn for a bit success could be just around the corner."

"Were there unwritten rules?"

"Well, you tried to keep within the law, but I saw people who did whatever was necessary to make their next million. If you want to make serious money, then it has to be your number one priority over everything else – family, friends, morals. It was a very different world to your working life, James."

"I can imagine."

James wondered again about his brother and how much trouble he was in. He was even more convinced that Peter's situation was not just about the normal cut and thrust of business life. It was likely to be something much more questionable. He was tempted to speak more openly with Stan about his brother but resisted for the moment. He appreciated Stan's concern for him and was pleased to have him around.

"Do you ever regret going into business?"

"No, I did very well out of it. I wished I'd done certain things differently, of course – don't we all? And it probably took up too much of my life which could explain why I'm still single. But no, it was a good choice for me. I liked the challenge and I had the drive to make it work."

James couldn't imagine making it in business. He felt rather naïve about the workings of such a different world. He really wasn't sure what he could do if he were no longer a vicar. He didn't have an obvious skill like Simon and the business world would probably laugh at his rather reflective approach to life. Perhaps he could do an online careers guidance questionnaire. He thought back to the careers advice he'd got at school. Was it time to train as a librarian? He knew Alice often went to the local library, so at least there would be that potential bonus.

"Are you okay, vicar?" Stan asked.

"Yes, sorry, miles away," James shrugged and smiled. "But thank you for the money again. I'm looking into what I can spend it on."

"Well, make sure you spend it on yourself. You look like you need a break."

CHAPTER 27

"So, if you weren't a vicar, what do you think you would be?"

Alice always seemed to hit on the most pertinent questions, James reflected, as they sat down again to discuss the life of a church minister. Of course it was a question he had been giving a lot of thought to recently but he seemed no nearer to getting an answer. To stall for time, he told Alice about Simon and how he had shown some design skills which could well be the key to his future career.

"That's great!" Alice said. "Your patience with him paid off."

"So maybe careers adviser then. I'd be able to help people and there'd be the satisfaction of setting people on a path that's right for them."

"Would you want to be a careers adviser?"

James paused. If he were honest, the prospect did not excite him. He could imagine a lot people would be difficult to advise. Maybe he had just struck lucky with Simon (although he would never say that to Simon as it would probably lead to an intense theological discussion about whether a Christian should use such a phrase).

"How are you two love birds?"

James' train of thought was interrupted by the arrival of Jack, clearly relishing how easy it was to embarrass the "Vic".

Alice smiled at him.

"Shouldn't you be at school?" she asked him.

"No, I'm happier when I'm not there and so are the teachers. So it's a win-win."

"It doesn't worry you that you'll leave education without any qualifications?" Alice asked.

"I already have. What they teach you isn't really going to help me. I'll never be able to write a history essay but, do you know, I can live with that."

"What will you do for a living?"

"I'll go into the family business. To be fair, I'm already in it. That's why I can afford this luxury hot chocolate."

"You're missing out on learning about the world, though. You know, learning for learning's sake. It doesn't all have to lead to a job."

"Yeah, maybe. I do think about that sometimes," Jack admitted. "But I think education's a bit wasted on teenagers. I'll probably do some classes or more likely online learning when I'm older. My dad is doing our family tree and it's really interesting to see what life was like a few generations back."

"Jack has a lot of qualities that will help him in business. He can relate to all sorts of people. And he's worldly-wise, for want of a better phrase," James observed.

"Well, thanks, Vic. I didn't realise you appreciated me so much. Shouldn't you be telling me to get back to school?"

"Yes, get back to school, you rebel," James said in his sternest voice.

Jack smiled.

"Sorry, mate, but I don't think you'd make a teacher. Anyway, I'll leave you to it. Though what you have to discuss with your regular meetings in here, I can't imagine. Unless of course....."

Alice decided to cut him off.

"We're talking about getting truants off the street, if you must know."

Jack smiled again as he departed.

"Well, good luck with that!"

James and Alice discussed whether Jack had a point and agreed that education is limited when it has a "one size fits all" approach. Alice appreciated the fact that James did not simply dismiss Jack as a rebellious truant but could see his qualities. As they talked further about what he might do if he were not a vicar, Alice mentioned Jeremy.

"What about the sort of work he does?" she asked. "Could you see yourself doing that?"

"I don't think so," James said. "I'm not good at carrying secrets around and I guess he probably has to be dishonest at times."

"For the sake of the country's security, no doubt."

James resented the fact that Alice saw his brother as some sort of hero, selflessly keeping us all safe. He tried to steer the conversation back to alternative careers but the relaxed and comfortable mood he usually enjoyed when talking to Alice was proving elusive today. He made his excuses to go and left Alice wondering again about the state of his mental health.

CHAPTER 28

Catching up with the cricket online as he finished his breakfast, James was quite looking forward to Simon's visit. He felt sure Simon's Away Day materials would look impressive and was pleased that their conversation would be much less awkward. Discovering Simon's talent for design had been a real breakthrough moment, a rare positive experience in a very trying period.

"Morning, bro!"

Peter had entered the kitchen without James noticing.

"Morning," James managed.

"Not full of the joy of the Lord this morning, then?"

James managed to control his temper and gave himself a moment to think before he responded.

"I'm fed up of covering for you. What's it like to lie whenever it suits you? You have no shame at all, do you?"

"Live in the real world, mate," Peter responded. "Everyone lies! And if it allows me to get to spend time with someone like Alice then bring it on!"

"What?"

"Yeah, she's really taken with this GCHQ idea. Bit of a brainwave on my part, don't you think? A job where you can't tell the truth because it may endanger government secrets. I've booked afternoon tea for the two of us so I can tell her all about this secret world."

Before James could react, the doorbell rang. He went to answer it while Peter moved out of sight in the kitchen.

"Good morning, Reverend Chambers."

Simon initially appeared to be his usual earnest self but there was something slightly more relaxed about his mood. He didn't smile – that would be going too far – but James sensed he was more comfortable with life. He invited him in and they went to his study to look at the Away Day materials. Simon's work was even better than James had expected. The handout that everyone would receive was clear and simple. There was space for notes and the layout almost made you want to write something in the space to make it your own. Simon had used the weighing scales image sparingly but effectively, and he had also produced printed versions of key passages that would be used in the discussion groups. James had been to many church events where the handouts had been a last-minute rush job on an ancient photocopier. This felt like the other end of the scale.

"This is all excellent, Simon!" James said with genuine enthusiasm.

"I think it looks reasonable," Simon agreed, "but obviously you and the committee must make the final decision. The materials should serve as a tool to support the message and promote discussion. And the emphasis is on support rather than distract from. There are other designs which might achieve that goal more effectively. If you have the time, you may like to consider alternative options."

To James' amazement, Simon opened his bag and took out two further sets of materials, each with its own style.

"This set focusses on the idea of light – the truth is made apparent by the light shining on it. The image is effective,

I believe, though I may have repeated it too many times. And with the final approach I have tried to get across the sense of freedom, based of course on Jesus' words, 'the truth will set you free.' This is perhaps the most obvious in terms of linking to the Bible, and of course it is always good to be reminded that the truth will set you free."

James tried to manage his thoughts. The irony of using a phrase about 'the truth setting you free' was not lost on him. Maybe he should come clean during the Church Away Day and just see what happened. And then there was his brother. James imagined Peter's afternoon tea with Alice. He knew his brother was very different from him. Peter could simply switch off from any chaos and disasters in his life and switch on the charm, and it was a charm which Alice enjoyed. He realised he had been hard work recently but Alice was the one person he felt totally comfortable with. If his brother spoilt that..... James felt a surge of anger.

"What are you thinking, Reverend Chambers?"

"What?"

"I understand there is a lot to take in with these designs, but I was wondering whether you had any initial opinions as to whether they would be a suitable vehicle for supporting the discussion and reflection on truth at the Away Day?"

James forced himself to get back to the task in hand.

"First of all, Simon, let me say how impressed I am with all of your work. I think we could use any of these on the day and everyone will believe we have spent money on a top designer."

"Thank you, Reverend Chambers. I am very encouraged to hear that. It is rare to hear such positive feedback on anything I do."

"Really?"

"Yes, my parents don't like to praise things I do in case I get big-headed."

"It's clear you have a talent here, Simon. Did you look at any of the courses on those websites we looked at?"

"I did. There is one that looks particularly interesting. I think I should pursue this rather than continue with the work shadowing, as long as you have no objection to that change in my course of action, Reverend Chambers."

"That's fine by me, Simon. In fact I think it's a very good decision."

CHAPTER 29

"So, which of these problems is causing you the most worry, would you say?"

James had decided to go and see the one person he could be completely open with. Bishop John listened intently as he talked about his loss of faith, his deceitful brother and his struggles with leading an Away Day on truth.

"I just feel so devious and dishonest the whole time. I don't think I can carry on like this," James explained.

"I could come along and help at the Away Day. A bishop needs to be involved with his churches and it's a long time since I've been to your parish."

"I think that would look odd. It's very last minute to announce the Bishop wanting to be involved. People would wonder what's going on. I expect some of them wonder that already."

The Bishop also revealed that he had a friend who worked at GCHQ. Maybe he could visit James and mention this in front of his brother. However, James was again unsure whether this would help. Knowing his brother, he would probably just lie his way out of the situation and carry on regardless.

"Do you ever have doubts?" James asked.

"Faith is based on spiritual conviction rather than proof, and that conviction does vary, yes," the Bishop admitted, "but I've never lost my faith."

"So where does that conviction come from?"

"Well, I'd have to say God, because I can't explain it any other way. My conversion experience was strong – it was a moment of real change for me, unexpected, and it made a lasting difference to the way I see life. Having said that, I know that not everyone has a conversion experience so people come to faith in different ways."

"But intellectually, how can you justify your faith?"

"It's a faith, a deeply held conviction. In my experience academic debates about faith tend to be like debates about politics – everyone arrives with their set view and nobody changes, and some people get very agitated along the way. So the views often end up being even more entrenched than they were at the start."

James was beginning to enjoy the opportunity to throw questions at the Bishop. His loss of faith and his desperation at the position he found himself in had given him an unexpected freedom.

"What about the argument that the beauty of the world shows a creator at work?"

"It's an argument. It may work for some people but I think the relationship argument is stronger."

"The relationship argument?"

"The deepest satisfaction in life comes through relationships – it could be family, friends, colleagues, other groups of people. It surpasses the other things people strive for – like success or achievement or material things. I hear it so often with older people looking back on their lives, their faces light up when they talk about certain people. I think that's a hint of why God made us."

"For a relationship with Him?"

"Yes. The start of the Bible shows man in perfect harmony with God and then we messed up. But that relationship can be rescued through Christ and what He did."

"So how do you describe your relationship with God to non-believers?"

"Now I see through a glass darkly."

James recognised the phrase from the New Testament; he had looked it up for the church evening about the reliability of the Bible. It was found in chapter 13 of Paul's first letter to the Corinthians, the great chapter about love.

"That's right," the Bishop continued. "We have an imperfect view in this life. At times it's just an inkling. But you know what we're like - we want to know everything."

"So how do you pray?"

"I tend to use the Lord's Prayer as a basis. It reminds us of who God is, it expresses our desire to be open to Him and shows an awareness of our own nature."

"Don't you ever pray about specific things or people?" James asked. "Have you prayed about me?"

"I have."

"Did you pray that I'd go off and be a librarian and stop causing you problems?"

Bishop John smiled.

"Surprisingly not. My prayers about people or situations tend to be less specific than that. It's more a case of asking God to work or guide in a particular situation and again acknowledging our dependence on Him. Do you want to be a librarian?"

"No."

"Okay. I won't pray that, then."

Now James smiled. He felt more relaxed than he had for a long time. It had been such a relief to talk to someone without having to maintain a lie. Nothing had been solved and he was returning to a life where he had to think carefully before he spoke to ensure he was not giving anything away. However his conversation with Bishop John had reminded him of how good it was to be open and honest with someone. He felt quite refreshed as he faced up to the challenges back in the parish.

CHAPTER 30

"So Jesus said, 'the truth will set you free.' He also described himself as the truth. It's an instruction to follow exactly what the Bible says. Regardless of what society says. I know lots of things have changed in two thousand years but people haven't changed and the Bible is about human nature."

Bernard was in his element. After the initial talk from John Turner, the Away Day guest speaker, the discussion groups were now in full flow. James had put a lot of thought into how to organise the groups, but in the end he had to accept that Bernard would dominate any group he found himself in. He loved the opportunity to express his views and interpretations and his tone was one which made people wary of disagreeing. So the discussion around the verses in the gospel of John chapter eight was in danger of turning into a monologue.

James' role was to wander between the groups, joining in when he felt it appropriate, though preferably not at all. As he listened to Bernard, he felt he needed to say something.

"I think the interesting thing here is the context of Jesus' words…" James started.

"Oh no, I hate that word 'context'," Bernard interrupted. "People use it to explain away all sorts of Biblical truths by saying they only applied at the time and that things have changed."

"Hold on a minute, Bernard. That's not at all what I'm saying. I think Jesus' words apply just as much today as they did then," James explained patiently. "He is speaking after the religious leaders of the time were dealing with a woman caught in adultery and they wanted to stone her, based on an Old Testament law. So Jesus turned the focus on the religious leaders and asked any of them who had never sinned to throw the first stone. Of course, they'd all sinned, so they had to turn away. So Jesus in effect set her free from the consequences of sin, symbolising what his mission was. Maybe when he talks about the truth setting people free, he's referring to the way he can set people free from condemnation."

"So was Jesus telling the religious leaders that their interpretation of the Old Testament instruction was wrong?"

Simon was in Bernard's discussion group and had found the courage to speak, emboldened by James' presence.

"Well, Jesus also said he didn't come to abolish the Old Testament law but to fulfil it," James continued. "I think his most interesting reference to the Old Testament rules is when he talks about the ten commandments; he makes it clear that two of them are greater than the others – love God and love others. If you keep those, everything else will fall into place. I think the religious leaders liked to get a bit legalistic and so Jesus made them look at things in a different way."

"That's all very well," said Bernard, "but you can't just say 'love everyone' and then we all go round smiling at each . other. That's not the real world. There's got to be some rules and guidelines so we know what's right. And the Bible is full of them."

"True," James agreed, "and the Biblical guidance on how we should live our lives is very important, but I think what Jesus may be getting at here is the attitude of heart of the religious leaders. They just wanted to point the finger and dish out punishment. I'm not sure they had a lot of love for the people they were leading."

"Not everyone goes round committing adultery," Bernard pointed out, keen not to appear to be backing down.

"Interestingly none of the religious leaders pointed that out," James replied. "They accepted that they had sinned and just walked away."

"Do you think that sexual sin is worse than other sin?"

Simon had again found the courage to speak and James enjoyed his directness when addressing Bernard. Before Bernard could reply, Simon continued with his thoughts and James was pleased to observe his new-found confidence.

"I think there is a tendency amongst some religious people to rank wrongdoings in order of seriousness, but I am not sure there is much in the Bible to justify doing so. In fact there is the simple statement that "all have sinned and fall short of the glory of God." It seems that sometimes we are more inclined to overlook greediness or selfishness or hypocrisy, than anything that involves sex. Yet I believe it is true that our selfish and greedy lifestyles in this part of the world cause a lot of misery."

As Bernard sat in reflective silence, James felt he could move on. Encouraging this particular discussion group to consider the next question, he left them and wandered over to another group. James was pleased to see Simon's growing confidence and was sure that the recognition of his design skills had been a part of that process. Several people had commented on the handouts and wondered how much they had cost. They had noticed the link with the powerpoint slides and it pleased James that Simon's skills were being recognised. James was delighted that Simon had a clear path ahead but couldn't help feeling the contrast with his own situation. Though the Away Day had so far gone as well as he could have hoped for, there were still many problems to face and he was no clearer about his own future.

After another talk from John Turner, a sociable lunch and further discussion groups, James brought the whole event together with an opportunity for people to say what they had gained from the day. There were many positive comments, some compliments about the organisation as well as reflections on the nature of truth. James was about to wind up the day by thanking everyone when Stan stood up to speak.

"I can't hold back on this any longer," he announced. "I think our vicar is hiding something. I don't know what it is but I have a bit of a sixth sense about these things. And I've had the impression for weeks he's holding something back. I think it's important we should know."

James was thrown by such a direct challenge. He had begun to relax, thinking that the day had gone far more smoothly than he had feared, and now Stan had put him on the spot in front of so many people. His breathing became more difficult and his throat tightened. Why would Stan do this now, in such a public way? For a brief moment James considered revealing the truth. It would completely overshadow all the positivity about the day and it could well undermine the sincerely-held faith of so many people who came to his church every week. This was not the time for life-changing confessions.

"Well, it's true that we don't reveal everything about ourselves to everyone," James managed after an awkwardly long silence.

He was aware his voice sounded strained but he managed to continue.

"That would be embarrassing or inappropriate or just plain boring … probably just plain boring in my case. I'm not sure you'd want to know how obsessed I am with the reflections of the England cricket selectors, for example, or the … the worries I have about my parents as they get older."

"Are you worried about your parents?" Stan asked.

"Not really, no," James admitted. "But I can assure you there is nothing for anyone to be concerned about. I think your question is motivated by concern, Stan, and I appreciate that but I can assure you that everything is fine. Yes, I can very much assure you of that."

James managed a few brief words of thanks, for the contributions of John Turner in particular, as well as the organising committee and Simon, and then he finished the day with a prayer. As people left, no one mentioned Stan's comments but he sensed in the handshakes and the concerned looks that, in spite of all the excellent teaching and discussion, the main question people were taking away from the day would be 'what is James hiding?'

CHAPTER 31

Deep in thought, James drove home on automatic pilot. It was one of those journeys where he would have no recollection of anything he passed or any other road users because his mind was full of thoughts about his troubling situation. He felt disappointed that Stan had chosen such a public occasion to confront him, aware that everyone would now sense he had an issue. He knew the gossipmongers would be speculating wildly. He couldn't stop his mind coming up with possibilities. He thought it unlikely they would guess he had simply lost his faith, but he felt it must have been obvious from his reaction to Stan's question that there was an issue. As a single man, he knew there were some who wondered about his sexual orientation, and people seemed to enjoy that sort of speculation. Others might be wondering whether James was planning some major change to the way the church was run; any changes to Sunday services would be met with resistance by large numbers of the congregation so this would also cause some concern. He just had to let them wonder until the time was right to announce his decision. However, he had an overwhelming sense of letting people down by continuing to play a role which felt like such a big lie.

As he turned into his drive, he noticed a car parked near his house. He immediately thought one of the church members who had attended the Away Day was so concerned they had driven straight round to see him. Tired and fraught, this was something he did not want to face. James parked and walked towards the visitor's car. A well-built man got out of the driver's side and an even larger man in dark glasses stepped out of the passenger side. James did not recognise them and felt slightly uneasy, especially when they approached him together. Neither of the men smiled and both looked at him intently.

"You James Chambers?" the driver asked.

His tone was blunt and menacing and his stare was unrelenting. James tried to remain calm.

"I am," he managed to say without too much nervousness in his voice. "And who are you?"

171

"Where's Peter?"

James immediately realised what was going on. He was now even more annoyed with himself for agreeing that his brother could stay; he had enough issues of his own without having to deal with angry people his brother had upset.

"I don't know. I've been out all day at a church event. He has been staying with me but I don't know where he is all the time."

"So he could be inside?"

"His car's not here, so I doubt it."

"Let's have a look."

"Sorry?"

"We're going inside."

James was not keen but the larger man in dark glasses stepped forward and he knew he had little choice. He took out his key and the two men followed him to the front door. They entered the silent house and James called his brother's name. There was no reply.

"Where's his room?" the driver asked.

James' hesitation was again met by a menacing step forward from the larger man. He led them both up the stairs. He knocked on the door of Peter's bedroom. When there was no reply, he went in, followed by the two men. They immediately began picking up papers, opening drawers and emptying the bag that Peter had left. James felt helpless as he watched.

"What are you looking for?"

There was no reply. However, it soon became apparent that their search had not been successful. The threatening mood emanating from the two men seemed to darken further.

"We'll look downstairs," the driver said.

James led them down and they continued their search in the lounge and then the kitchen, showing a particular interest in any pieces of paper lying around. They opened the kitchen cupboards to make sure nothing was hidden in them. The lack of success was clearly annoying the men.

"Where is he then?" the driver asked.

"Look, I've told you. I don't know where he goes. He doesn't tell me."

The larger man in the dark glasses swept his enormous arm across the table, sending the china teapot and mugs crashing to the floor. James was shocked and the feeling of fear made him tremble. His way out of the kitchen was blocked and these two men were clearly used to getting their own way, regardless of what it took.

"One last chance. Think harder."

"He's obviously thought about this," James managed, "and he hasn't told me anything. I honestly don't know."

"Phone him. Tell him he needs to get back here."

"He hasn't given me his number. I imagine he thought …."

James was unable to finish his sentence as the powerful punch to his stomach meant he could hardly breathe, let alone speak. He bent over, trying to catch his breath, and was caught by another fist to the face. The pain was excruciating – he was sure his head had been split open. In more pain than he had ever felt in his life, he fell to the floor. Drifting in and out of consciousness, he felt completely helpless. The boots landing further blows to his body felt like concrete blocks breaking his bones. He tried to speak but the feeble gurgling communicated nothing. Finally he passed out.

CHAPTER 32

The pain pulsing through his body was bad enough, but the sense that his head was held in a medieval torture device made James groan in desperation for some sort of relief. He sensed a figure nearby who was paying him some attention. Someone said something but the words weren't clear. Taking his time to work out where he was, he noticed there were bright lights and he could see the outline of some moving shapes. He was in bed and he did not dare move as he feared the pain would be excruciating. As his focus gradually returned, he was able to make out a pattern on the wall opposite. Fairly bland and in need of fresh paint, it suggested an uncared-for room which he couldn't place. He considered the option of turning his head to take in more of the scene but quickly rejected this at the thought of the torment it might cause him.

As he struggled to piece together what was going on, a shape came into view, not far from his face. Working through the pain, he forced himself to focus and realised it was Alice, leaning over him.

"Morning, James."

To see Alice and to hear her voice seemed to take the edge off his suffering. He wanted to respond but he worried about what the effort would do to him. He looked at her; in fact he stared at her. With Alice's face hovering above him and James not daring to move, he had no choice and this seemed to lift his mood too.

"You're in hospital."

James tried to respond but he produced little more than an incomprehensible gurgle. Alice smiled.

"I'll take that as a 'good morning'."

James gurgled again and this time it sounded more like a recognisable phrase.

"And I'll take that as 'how are you?'" said Alice. "I'm okay, thanks. Certainly a lot better than you. You were attacked. Your friend Jeremy found you on the kitchen floor when he got home. Do you remember any of it?"

James started to shake his head but immediately regretted it, the shooting pains across his forehead making him wince.

"Sorry, James," Alice said. "Don't worry about responding. I shouldn't ask you questions. In fact I had trouble persuading them to let me see you at all. You took quite a beating. The good news is you should recover but in the short term you'll be living off pain killers. Severe bruising, concussion and a couple of broken ribs. Somebody wasn't happy with you…. And I'd heard the Away Day had gone very well." James wasn't ready to respond to jokes but he was enjoying having Alice at his bedside. The mention of the Away Day helped to bring back some memories, the pain returning as he recalled the two men on his doorstep.

"Sorry, James. I shouldn't joke. This was obviously something serious and the police are involved."

James noticed movement behind Alice and then she disappeared from his field of vision. He attempted to move his head slightly to one side and was pleased to be able to do so without causing unbearable pain. He could see a nurse talking to Alice. Their expressions were serious and the nurse looked particularly stern. Alice returned to lean over James again.

"I'm going to have to go, James. You need plenty of rest. They're pleased with how you're progressing and I don't want to be responsible for any setback. I'll come and see you again and then we can talk."

Alice gave a little wave and then disappeared from view. James felt better for having seen her and the events which led to his hospitalisation were coming back to him. However, her parting words stuck with him – what did she mean by "we can talk"? What would they talk about? He felt it was a strange thing to say, as if they had something significant to sort out. He was wondering whether he was reading too much into Alice's words when the nurse came over and encouraged him to sleep. James realised his body was exhausted from this brief interaction and he was happy to relax back into the pillow and do as he was told. He just made out the nurse's words as he drifted off.

"She was very keen to see you. But no more visitors now for a couple of days."

CHAPTER 33

"Yo, gangster Vic!"

James had been dozing but was now awake as he realised that Jack was standing at the end of his bed. Those 'couple of days' must have passed in a haze of painkillers.

"You been nicking converts from someone else's patch? So they send round the God squad to rough you up?"

James had to smile – inwardly at least; he wasn't sure his face was registering a normal range of emotions as yet, although he was making good progress with his recovery (as the nurses kept telling him).

"I hear you've been a naughty vicar," Jack was speaking in a comedy villain voice and clearly enjoying himself.

"That's not what they said," James managed to croak.

His voice was getting back to normal, though he was a little nervous about using it. The nurses were encouraging him to push himself in his recovery and James was doing his best.

"Were they wearing dog collars?" Jack asked.

"No, they were in disguise," James replied with another attempt at a smile. "And how are you, Jack?"

Jack was as cheerful as ever. He explained that as soon as Alice told him about the attack, he had come straight to the hospital. And he was missing double maths so that he could be here.

"When did you last go to double maths?" James asked.

"Yeah, that's a fair question, Vic. When did I last go to any maths lesson? That's also a fair question."

As they chatted, one of the nurses came in to check the machines at the side of James' bed.

"Good to see your brother, eh, James?" she said as she noted down some figures.

James didn't respond. His brother? What did the nurse know? Had Peter stopped pretending to be Jeremy? Did everyone now know he'd been lying to them about

Peter? Perhaps he had been in to visit and James had lost all memory of it. Before he could think of something to say, Jack chipped in.

"Always good to see each other."

"That's good," the nurse said as she was leaving. "You need the support of family at a time like this."

Once the nurse had gone, Jack explained that he didn't think they would let 'some random teenage truant' in to visit, so he told them he was Jack Chambers, James' younger brother. He quite liked the sound of it.

"I also told them how you used to nick all my sweets when I was little. You know, just to make it sound real."

"Great," James managed, though he was actually quite touched that Jack had gone to such lengths to visit. "But thanks for making the effort."

"That's all right, Vic. It's one of the advantages of being a persistent truant, you've got the time to do these sorts of things."

James had to smile again.

"What are you going to do with your life, Jack?"

"Whoa, what's with the big questions, Vic? Just see what each day brings and go with the flow."

James realised he did not have the energy for a lengthy discussion so he did not respond. However, he spent a few moments thinking about Jack's response. His approach to life was all very well when you were a teenager and someone else was providing a roof over your head but at some point you had to take some responsibility. On the other hand there was a tendency as an adult to want everything sorted, probably born of a desire for control, for knowing where life was going. The last few weeks had taught James that the feeling of having things sorted and being in control was often an illusion. He closed his eyes as he thought of the situations in his life that were still far from sorted.

"So did you manage to land a few punches?" Jack asked.

James opened his eyes.

"There were two of them. They were bigger than me. And I wasn't expecting it."

"Excuses, excuses."

The nurse entered again and Jack took the hint that James was getting tired and it was time to leave.

"Look after yourself, bro," he said as he left the room.

James dozed again as he thought about the dishonesty of his real brother, the hypocrisy of carrying on as a vicar and his tense relationship with Alice. Maybe life was easier as a teenage truant.

CHAPTER 34

"You said some interesting things when you were first coming round."

The following day Alice was visiting again, looking at him from the chair next to his bed. James was sitting up and for the first time beginning to think he was making progress in his recovery. He could move his head without wanting to scream and, as long as he kept the painkillers topped up, he could almost ignore his injuries and focus on other issues. He had even caught up with the cricket scores and had spent some time thinking about the selection issues facing England in the forthcoming Test series. However, he suspected Alice was not referring to his thoughts on who should play wicketkeeper. He remembered she had said they would be able to talk once James was feeling better. He sensed that time had arrived.

"Did I?"

"Yes, interesting things about your faith."

"Well, I am a vicar, after all."

"Hmm," said Alice, "that's the thing. You would expect a vicar to have a faith. Not wondering whether it was 'wishful thinking supported by centuries of tradition.'"

James was annoyed that he was having to deal with this now. And he was even more annoyed at his brother. If he hadn't turned up, James wouldn't have been attacked by a couple of heavies and he wouldn't be in this position now. He decided to be cagey.

"It's always good to examine opposing viewpoints. I've watched Richard Dawkins on YouTube, you know. It keeps you on your toes."

"It didn't sound like you were examining a viewpoint. You talked about delivering a sermon and then thinking at the end of it that your faith had gone."

There was a long silence. Both James and Alice reflected on the situation he found himself in. James tried to work out exactly how he was feeling. After weeks of covering up his loss of faith, there was a sense of relief that it was now out in the open, at least with Alice. On the other hand James faced the challenge of starting a whole new career in his thirties, and he would struggle to explain all of this to his loyal parishioners. Maybe he would be responsible for some of them losing their faith too. Overall he still felt very out of control.

James then thought about the other lies in his life and wondered whether to tell Alice the whole truth; she would probably find out about them herself anyway, what with her journalistic instincts. Maybe she had turned up at the hospital as he was coming round in the hope of picking up some interesting information. James immediately felt bad about having such a negative view of Alice and dismissed this idea.

"It could explain why you've been so different recently," Alice said. "But maybe doubts are part of the deal when you have a faith?"

"Have you been researching doubting Thomas?"

"No. But it's not a straightforward thing, faith, is it? I know it's a cliché but people do talk about it as a journey."

James did not respond. He was really unsure of the way ahead but he was beginning to enjoy again the familiar feeling of spending time with Alice. He was keen to prolong this visit and now he was beginning to feel a bit better, the nurses would have no objection.

"So, what have you been up to?"

"Oh, you know, working on articles. As usual."

"A day in the life of a vicar?"

"I was thinking of shelving that one. But now I come to think about it – a vicar who gets beaten up – that could be an interesting angle."

James wondered for a moment if Alice had taken photos of him while he was still unconscious to go with her article, but he quickly decided she would never do that.

"And then there's the Jeremy article," James said.

"Yes, Jeremy. Do you know much about his work at GCHQ?"

"Absolutely nothing."

James wondered whether he'd been talking about his brother in his semi-conscious state. In fact he almost hoped he had – then everyone would know the truth and he couldn't be blamed for it. Alice told him he hadn't mentioned Jeremy.

"I like him and he's got a lot of charm but I just sense there's something about him which doesn't quite ring true. He spoke about GCHQ as if he knew it from films or documentaries and he loved telling me there were secrets that only he knew. I think someone from GCHQ would be a bit more, I don't know … mature. Is he someone you trust?"

"Well, we all have our secrets," James replied.

"That's certainly true, vicar."

Once Alice left James to the quiet beeping of his hospital room, he realised again how out of control his life was. He wondered what Alice would do with the knowledge she now had of his lack of faith. He was quite confident she wouldn't write about it, but if she happened to mention it to anyone, he would never be able to go back to his church. There was no way he could get on his knees but James once again thought there would be nothing to lose by praying. And once again he was honest and told God he had no idea what to do.

CHAPTER 35

Having been allowed home after an assessment by the doctor, James now had the challenge of limiting visitors. He appreciated the concern of his parishioners but could not face a whole series of conversations based on half-truths at best. He regularly used the excuse of getting rest ("doctor's orders") and was able to put off most of the well-meaning people who had brought him flowers or cooked him lasagne. However, Stan was particularly persistent and had the excuse of being there to work on the garden. James had tried to turn him away but Stan insisted they needed to talk. His tone suggested there was no point in arguing.

"You've got to be honest with yourself, James," Stan began as they sat at the kitchen table. "Sometimes you need other people and they can help you in ways you don't expect."

James wondered what Stan was referring to. Perhaps Alice had talked to him and told him about their non-believing vicar.

"When I heard about you getting beaten up, I reckoned it must be to do with your mate," Stan continued. "I'd never been sure about him so I tracked him down for a little chat."

"A little chat?"

"In a manner of speaking. He's a bit of a wimp, actually. He must be, what, twenty years younger than me but I just grabbed him by the collar and he was shaking like a leaf."

"What did he tell you?"

"He told me about the guy he'd upset. He's involved in some very dubious stuff, your mate. I wished I'd gone with my instinct earlier. It could have saved you that session with the heavies."

"That would have been nice."

"Not much of a friend, your mate, Jeremy, is he?"

"Actually, he's not a friend and he's not Jeremy."

"What?"

"He's my brother, Peter."

Once again James had that sense of relief that came with telling the truth. Perhaps he should have been honest much sooner, or just refused from the start to cover for Peter's lies. Would he be in a better situation now? What if Peter had been hunted down and attacked after James had sent him away? Would that be worse? Stan was nodding.

"Right! I can see now why you played along. Your own brother! You're very different, aren't you? He owes you big time. But somehow I suspect he hasn't really thought about that, has he?"

James felt better for Stan's support. Maybe he was right about sharing concerns. Certainly in this case Stan could have been a big help. James wondered whether he would have responded differently if he hadn't been a vicar. A church minister is in a strange situation. There is a pressure to feel like he has everything sorted, and it would have been difficult to have shared any of the issues he had been struggling with. However, as Stan had made clear, it would have been useful to talk them over with someone. Another perspective can sometimes come up with solutions you hadn't realised existed.

James' mobile rang and he saw it was Bishop John. James was ignoring most calls but he felt he ought to speak to the Bishop, who was no doubt concerned about his welfare. In fact the Bishop was eager to see him and wondered whether he could call in today. James was not especially keen. He got tired quite quickly and he realised the Bishop would want to talk about his future.

"It would be good to see you again, James," Bishop John said. "I'm hoping you look a bit better than you did when I visited the hospital. That was not a great sight."

"Yes, I'm on the mend, thanks," James replied.

"That's good to hear. Don't worry about getting anything in. I'll just have a cup of tea. And we can chat over a few things."

James explained the situation to Stan who took the hint to leave.

"Let me know if you need anything," Stan said as he left. "Anything at all."

"Thanks for your support, Stan."

As James was left alone, he wondered about Bishop John's words. What 'few things' did he want to 'chat over'? Maybe James was reading too much into a throwaway phrase, but he wondered whether the Bishop had reached a decision about his future.

CHAPTER 36

"So, which sermon do you think upset these two men?"

Bishop John was trying to break the ice with a joke and James laughed politely. As he sipped his tea, he decided he might as well explain the situation with his brother and so he told John the truth about the reason for the beating.

"You really have been through a tough time, haven't you?"

"Yes, but it's actually a relief being able to talk honestly about this. Finally. It's hard work covering up the truth."

"Hm. That's what I want to talk to you about, actually. I've had a visit from someone in your parish."

"Really? Who?"

"Well, they didn't want me to tell you."

James knew it had to be Alice. She'd heard the truth about his faith and obviously felt the Bishop needed to know. It was entirely understandable – if you discover your vicar's an atheist, it's fair enough to point out he shouldn't be in the job. However, James was still surprised she'd gone to see the Bishop so quickly.

"Is she threatening to write an article about a vicar with no faith?"

"No, it's not that..."

"Maybe the dishonesty of the church."

"I think you've worked out who it is. And she's not planning any articles."

James was relieved. He could accept leaving the church but did not want to be known as the vicar who lived out a fake faith. He waited for Bishop John to tell him it was time to hand in his resignation.

"She thinks I should encourage you to carry on as a church minister."

James could not believe what he was hearing. He stared at Bishop John, desperately trying to process what was going on.

"She said that?"

"She did."

Maybe it wasn't Alice who had visited the Bishop and they were talking at cross purposes.

"Very attractive woman with black hair? Late twenties?" James asked.

"That's right. Name of Alice. She used an image about your being in a big pothole in the journey of faith – I quite liked that phrase, I think I might use it myself. But she thinks you'll come out of it stronger. She talked about faith being on a spectrum – there's ideas and principles at one end and then a relationship with God at the other. We agreed you need the principles, the doctrine, if you like – that supports the relationship – but she thinks you've been a bit too near the ideas end."

"She said all that?"

"Yes, she's a bit of a thinker, I'd say. She reckons the challenges you've been facing might just move you along that spectrum a bit. In a good way. Rather appropriately, it reminded me of that bit in the letter of James in the Bible – 'draw near to God and He will draw near to you'."

James could not hide his delight. After expecting the worst, the thought that Alice had said positive things about him made his spirits soar. And her words seemed to make sense of his situation. As the sun shone through the windows in his lounge, his mood was brighter than it had been for weeks.

"I think she's a bit of a fan of yours," Bishop John added.

As they discussed the way ahead for James, he couldn't stop himself breaking into a smile. He thought he had ruined his relationship with Alice after her discovery that he'd been living a lie. So to hear that she was actually on his side was wonderfully unexpected.

James tried to listen as the Bishop explained the way ahead. He thought James should take a couple of months off. The parish would understand as he had been attacked. And this would allow him time to consider his faith. James thought this sounded like a great plan. Maybe there was something in what Alice said. He had always loved debating ideas; perhaps he was too focussed on that. Maybe those simple prayers he'd managed were being answered. Faith as a daily dependence on God – rather than having everything 'sorted' – for the first time James had an inkling that there could be a way ahead.

"So you think I should carry on in the ministry?"

"Yes, I do."

"But I don't have all the answers."

"Do you think anyone does?"

"Probably not – if they're being honest."

"You've learnt a lot through this episode. The idea that faith is a relationship with God, through what Jesus has done – it's not new and it's really simple but we all need reminding of it when we get a bit too bogged down in theology and the need for answers. And we have to be open to the unexpected, rather than having everything under control."

James reflected for a moment.

"I remember C. S. Lewis talking about the numinous," he said, "something indefinable, inexplicable, which ends up in awe and wonder."

"Yes, if your faith is just ideas and principles and explanations, you might as well call it philosophy. Faith is more than that."

Bishop John was happy to sit in silence as James processed these ideas. He felt he was still learning about his faith. Maybe he always would be. The feeling that it was worth carrying on was getting stronger by the minute.

James finally sat up and for the first time in weeks he looked like someone who was ready to move on. He took another sip of tea.

"Do you think Alice would be willing to see me?" James asked Bishop John, suddenly concerned that Alice was just being kind to him, getting him back on his feet before she went off to lead her own life.

"I don't know," John said. "But if you do catch up with her, tell her I'm sorry I failed to keep her anonymous."

James was so grateful he hadn't – and so excited about catching up with Alice. After all that had happened he realised he could be completely honest with her and he couldn't wait.

CHAPTER 37

Waiting at his favourite table in the coffee shop, James couldn't remember ever feeling so nervous. Alice had agreed to meet up but he could not tell from her texts how the conversation would go. Would this be the time where they rounded off their friendship, wished each other well and went their separate ways? This was not what he wanted. However, he thought Alice might have lost respect for him because of the way he'd handled things. He couldn't bear the prospect of not having her in his life.

As Alice approached, he was struck again by her beauty. He stood up to greet her and she smiled briefly. His heart was racing. He thought of the doctor at the hospital who had told him to avoid stressful situations for a while. Some things were more important than a doctor's advice.

"Morning, James," she said.

"Morning, Alice. I've got the coffees. It's really good to see you. Really good."

"Thank you."

"I just want to say sorry," James began.

"You do?"

"Yes, I'm sorry I handled the last few weeks the way I did. I wasn't as honest as I should have been and I was quite short with you. I feel very bad about that."

"That was about Jeremy, wasn't it?"

James nodded.

They each studied their coffee for a moment. James was trying to work out which way this would go. He desperately wanted to get back to the relationship they'd had before his life became so complicated. Alice broke the silence.

"I feel a bit stupid for having been charmed by Jeremy. I suspect he's actually not very nice."

James nodded again.

"Are you good friends?"

"We're not friends."

"Sorry?"

"We're brothers. And his name's Peter."

"What?"

James explained the whole situation with Peter; his unexpected arrival, how he'd lied to cover for him and how he'd ended up in hospital because of him. Alice could not hide her surprise.

"How much covering up is there in your life?"

"Too much. I need to get it sorted. It's very hard work living a lie, week in, week out. I'm sorry I misled you about so much."

"Well, I suppose I can understand your not being open about a crisis of faith. You can't really tell everyone about that in your position. But why did you agree to my writing an article about you?"

At this moment Jack walked past the coffee shop window. He gave James a wave and then pointed at Alice, giving a double thumbs up gesture. For one horrible moment James thought he was coming in but thankfully he moved on.

"It was, well, it was a way of spending time with you. And I really like spending time with you. And I'm so glad I can finally be open and honest with you."

"Thank you," Alice said.

James couldn't work out whether there was fondness or sadness in her eyes.

"I didn't see this coming at all. This crisis of faith and then my brother landing on the doorstep hoping some thug wouldn't track him down. I suppose you never see these things coming, do you? You're going along quite smoothly and then suddenly …. you find yourself in a big pothole."

Alice stared at James, the hint of a smile on her face.

"The Bishop's been to see you, hasn't he?"

"Maybe."

"I knew I couldn't trust him."

"He sends his apologies - but he stood little chance in the face of my interrogation."

"So what are you going to do?"

James explained the Bishop's plan for him to take a couple of months off. The Bishop would announce that James needed the time to recover after the attack. However, they both knew he also needed the time to sort out where he stood on matters of faith.

"You sounded pretty clear in hospital."

"I was heavily sedated."

"You think that sort of excuse works at the gates of heaven?"

"I don't know. There's nothing in the Bible about denying your faith whilst under the influence of buprenorphine."

"That's a fair point."

James was pleased they were able to add a lighter note to the discussion. However, he was keen to bring up what Alice had said to the Bishop as he felt there might be some truth in it which could help him find a way forward.

"But there is something in the Bible about 'seeing through a glass darkly'. We want to know everything now, see everything clearly, have answers to all our questions, but

I'm not sure we can – not in this life. Your spectrum chat was interesting."

"'Spectrum chat'? Is that what the Bishop called it."

"Not exactly. But he was clearly taken with it. I reckon he might start quoting you so you can expect royalties."

"From the Church of England? That will just about cover a cup of coffee. Would you like another?"

James watched as Alice went to the counter. He hadn't felt this happy in weeks. It was such a great relief that he could finally be honest. And he loved being with this woman.

"So where did the spectrum idea come from?" James asked as Alice returned with the drinks.

"I found it on a discarded scrap of paper at a motorway service station near Ipswich."

"There are no motorway service stations near Ipswich. In fact there are no motorways near Ipswich. Now, if you'd said the A12, I might have believed you."

They both smiled.

"Have you got a serious answer?" James asked.

"If you look at the Garden of Eden story – whether you take it as literal or symbolic – it's all about relationships. It describes God wanting to create man and then the man needed someone else around. The greatest joy in life comes from relationships and it's as if that is from God. Look at what Jesus said when he was asked about how to pray. He came out with the Lord's Prayer – it starts with 'our Father in heaven' – it's a prayer of openness and dependency. And what Jesus did enables us to have that relationship. Of course it's not perfect in this life and we're learning all the time. And it can be a struggle when life is tough."

James reflected on what Alice had said. He'd been through a great deal since that Sunday morning where he felt he'd lost his faith. Maybe he needed to experience this challenging time to get to the point where he could continue his journey. Sitting in comfortable silence with Alice, he realised he'd now reached that point. He was ready to continue with his faith; it was as if the last few weeks had been a necessary time of reviewing and refining what he believed. Maybe Bishop John had sensed all along that this would happen. James thought back to that awful moment at the bottom of the pulpit steps and realised he had moved on a lot. He could now say to himself, "No. My faith hasn't gone.*"

"You're very quiet," Alice said.

"You've given me a lot to think about. And I'm in a big pothole, of course."

"Not traditionally known as quiet places."

"Maybe it's not so much quiet as lonely."

"I see."

"I've been thinking, Alice. I know I've been devious and rude to you but you are actually the person in the world I most like spending time with. You make me laugh, you make me think and I really value your opinion. If you'd come here this morning and told me you'd never wanted to see me again, I would have been completely broken. I think you're absolutely amazing. I want to be with you because ... because I love you."

"Are you inviting me to join you in your pothole?"

"I would really love that."

They gazed at each other. Alice reached across and placed her hand on his. Her smile made James as happy as he'd ever been.

WHEN JAMES STOPPED BELIEVING

Printed in Poland
by Amazon Fulfillment
Poland Sp. z o.o., Wrocław

65698224R00123